MW01123229

WOMEN WRITING FROM SMALL PLACES

Outskirts

WOMEN WRITING FROM SMALL PLACES

SHORT FICTION

EDITED BY

E MILY S CHULTZ

SUMACH
PRESS

NATIONAL LIBRARY OF CANADA
CATALOGUING IN PUBLICATION DATA

Main entry under title:
Outskirts: women writing from small places

ISBN 1-894549-13-9

1. Short stories, Canadian (English) — Women authors.
2. Canadian fiction (English) — Women authors. 3. Canadian
fiction (English) — 20th century. I. Schultz, Emily, 1974-
PS8321.087 2002   C813'.01089287   C2002-900861-1
PR9197.32.087 2002

*Sumach Press acknowledges the support
of the Ontario Arts Council and The Canada Council for the Arts
for our publishing program.*

Printed and bound in Canada

Published by
SUMACH PRESS
1415 Bathurst St., Suite 202
Toronto, Ontario Canada
M5R 3H8

www.sumachpress.com

This book is for my mother,
who just sorted her childhood home —
two centuries of family history —
deciding what to sell, what to give away,
and what to keep.

This Far

Helen Humphreys

Over the bridge. The iron railing.
Darkness plunges in slow, sad arcs
into the river below.
Nothing on the radio, just the tick
of a stone in the tire, the miles of it
wearing down. Imagined blue, that's
the sound of loss. Blue stone.

What are the things that make us
feel like who we are? Voices
in a room. A place to come from,
the bright, glittering wash of a city.
Landscape spliced to language.
Roads we know.

There's a stutter of light in the hall
behind us. Put on your coat, I say.
Dawn sticky red over the long cant of roofs.
The car door salted with frost. This is how
I come back, and leave, and never go.

"This Far" reprinted from Helen Humphreys, *Anthem* (1999)
with permission of Brick Books, London, Ontario.

Contents

INTRODUCTION

Outskirts is an anthology that gives rural women a voice, and a thoroughly unexpected one. Our houses and the houses of our neighbours are ordinary structures, and within them the most extraordinary emotions come to surface. Lovers dance around one another, waiting, biding their time for the right moment to ask the simplest questions. Over dinner, fathers chew on their daughters, while masticating red meat and tender white shoots of asparagus. Outside, the grass grows up through the bones of animals who couldn't make it, and we wonder what will happen to us if we aren't strong enough.

Fifteen exciting writers represent their homes through short fiction. From Canada's East Coast to West Coast, and as far north as Nunavut, these stories evoke a sense of place and purpose. Rather than repeat the realities of life in small towns, these stories represent how we *feel* about living there, not to mention the struggles involved in just being alive.

This project really took root in me after reading an issue of Canada's literary journal *Prism International* devoted to writers from Australia. Those stories were so evocative of place that even in the midst of a downtown Toronto winter, they stayed with me. There was a scene in one story in which five characters use the same sugar spoon to stir their coffees. To me, this moment defined place and character very clearly as one and the same; the smallest gestures we make can show who we are and where we come from. This made me want to edit a collection packed full of blunt poetry, moments demonstrative of both poverty and acceptance.

At the same time, I had fantasies of myself as the editor of a collection of hip, edgy young fiction. Yes, yet another collection of hip, edgy literature to stockpile next to the others which emerge each year in Canadian publishing. I realize now that this was a very *Toronto* kind of desire in me, a desire to be fashionable in my literary selections. And that might have been fine too, but this project called for something else, something subtler that I didn't really understand until the stories came in whispering it.

I could not predict the scope of the writing that would be submitted on the basis of a few classifieds, flyers, and Internet postings. What filtered in, slowly, through the mail were stories of a candid, yet quiet nature — stories with far more depth than I had even thought to solicit. From writers of varying ages, both established and emerging, these voices begged to be pressed side-by-side in spite of their differences. Solid, stoic, frank, and unafraid, these stories speak particularly to generation, to sex and death, animals and ancestry, to the passing on of flesh and blood in a world of water and stone.

How affected is the human experience by place, home, landscape? Beyond the grey cityscape of "gritty urban fiction" there is *Outskirts*, a collection which, I hope, will make the urban seem urbane. Collected here is a wave of writers who are coming into their own. All were born outside of Canada's urban centres, and most continue to live in small places. The authors explore the ways in which self and environment shift and grow together. Without pretension, they document the human experience and make some of the baser elements of our lives unfathomably lovely.

Emily Schultz
Toronto
February 2002

"*N. Loves Peggy*"

KELLY COOPER

JARVIS AND I grew up on farms south of Eyehill, a town of about
a hundred and twenty, no bank, no hospital, no high school.
We shared a sense of destiny and not much else. And even that
showed itself differently. Jarvis was always on the lookout, restless, searching for it. I turned inward and waited. Drove him
crazy. "You want to stay here all your life?" he'd demand.

"No."

"Well?"

I said nothing, developed patterns of silence, knowing my
refusal to answer drove him craziest of all.

Reading on the school bus makes me feel sick, but I do it anyway
because a book is a good way to ignore Jarvis. After grade nine,
Eyehill sends its children to a larger school in a much larger
town twenty-five miles away. During the last fifteen minutes of
the route, he and I are the only ones left on the bus. This is
when he wants to have conversations. We don't have much to do
with each other at school. For one thing, he's a year older, part
of a large intimidating group of boys who line up with their backs
against the hallway walls, judging the girls unlucky enough or

bold enough to walk that gauntlet. For another, I'm no use to him.

Jarvis is the king of one-night stands, and as well an obvious social climber. He picks up easy girls at parties and takes them outside for an hour or so, but never asks them on dates. The girls he does ask out are the popular ones: pretty girls, girls on the volleyball team, exotic girls from foreign countries who are on exchange programs at our school. When one of them says yes, then he really thinks he's done something, Jarvis from a hick town like Eyehill getting a date with a girl at the top of the ladder. It's all sex and status with him. I, on the other hand, am not interested in matters of the flesh. I am interested in ideas. I read poetry that doesn't rhyme and no one asks me out.

The book giving me motion sickness today is *The Edible Woman.* My English teacher, Ms. Sloan, gave it to me. *I went to school with Margaret Atwood,* she said, *no one suspected what she would become. We called her Peggy then.*

"Good book?" he asks.

"It's Atwood," I say.

"I thought from the title it might be a dirty book. Any good parts like that?"

"It's not dirty. It's Literature." Then I tell him the story of Ms. Sloan and Margaret Atwood and how she was just Peggy.

"Neil Young sings a song about a girl called Peggy."

"Who's Neil Young?"

Jarvis hangs out with a bunch of older guys. One of them owns a house in town. They sit around listening to music from the sixties. My mother thinks they smoke drugs. They probably do.

"You don't know Neil Young? Talk about out of it."

I ignore him, knowing he wants a reaction. The bus bounces over ruts. The lines of print on the page move up and down like a print-out from one of those machines I've seen on detective shows, the ones that are supposed to detect lies. It seems the conversation is over until he asks, "How old's this Atwood?"

"Forty-five." I know this because of a report I'd written a few months earlier. Biography of a Canadian Writer.

"She's older than he is. Young guys like older women. Where's she from?"

"Ontario." ... *she came to know intimately the bush country of Northern Ontario,* the biography said.

"See. I knew it. Some of Neil Young's first gigs were in Northern Ontario. I bet they had a thing going." He hums for a mile or two before saying, "She left him, probably. Broke his heart. Typical woman."

I just look down at the book, pretending to read. He's staring at me, but I won't look back. I tell myself I am not interested in the way my skin can suddenly feel the brush of every thread in the weave of my shirt. I don't care about how, without even looking at him, I know his hand is only two inches away from my shoulder.

"You'll never get anywhere," Jarvis says, "you've got no imagination."

Not long after that, I start seeing Jarvis six days a week instead of five. It is spring, the calving season, and my father hires him to work on Saturdays because there are a lot of sick calves that require treatment, a shot of antibiotic for pneumonia. We try to sneak up on them when they are sleeping in the late April sunshine, but if this doesn't work, we have to chase them into a corner. I grab a calf's hind leg and pull. It hops backwards on three legs until Jarvis throws it on its side and pins it to the ground, holding the legs immobile while I jab the needle into the soft fold of skin where the animal's neck meets its shoulder.

One morning, a cow from the pasture close to the house comes to the feed trough with bloody shreds hanging from under her tail, but no calf in sight. Jarvis and I are sent on foot to search for the missing animal. I hate the thought of finding it dead, stretched out on a hilltop maybe, where the ground is warm enough for crocuses and everything with leaves is rising, but the calf just lays there, flat. In a few months the grass will grow through the gaps in its bones. I hate it the most when the cow won't leave it, some of them stay for two or three days with a dead calf, licking it, wild-eyed and ready to defend, driven by a fearsome kind of love.

Half an hour of looking, and we still haven't found it. We walked the bush by the lake three times and the whole pasture once, which isn't easy because most of it is hillside, marked by stones and gullies. Sun warms the rocks and I sit on a large one. Jarvis, who doesn't care about damp ground, stretches out on the grass beside me. It is warm enough to be without coats, without a sweatshirt even, so I take mine off and enjoy the sun on my arms. The first T-shirt day of the year.

"It's got to be somewhere in the bush," I say. "Are you sure you checked right down to the water?"

He doesn't answer, so I look at him, lying there with his arm raised up to block the sun, his eyes closed. I reach out to poke him in the ribs or push against his bent knee, to make the kind of contact we've made for years, but something happens. The clear, warm light strikes the metal of his belt buckle. My fingers relax, no longer stiff above a hand flat-palmed for striking. They drift down and lay gentle on the buckle. I feel the slight shift of his body, a tightening of muscle. Now he's staring at me, a band of shadow across his eyes like a mask. I look at the blue shirt that covers his flat stomach, look lower, then up again at the hand resting between the two places, the hand that seems part of someone else, not mine at all. He moves his arm and curves his fingers around my wrist without pressure, does not guide my hand further or push it away. The smell of new leaves blows up from the bush by the lake. Sweet. I feel the rise and fall of Jarvis breathing, once, twice, is the air as sweet for him? I lift my hand away and Jarvis lets me go.

"Did you check right down to the water?" I ask again, rough-voiced, as if I hadn't touched him.

We find the calf. All we can see are its ears. The cow had given birth at the edge of a deep narrow gully full of meltwater and winter snow. The calf had slipped down into it, and been buried up to its neck. We pull it out. Alive. Jarvis carries it home on his shoulders, not talking for once, both of us quiet beneath the weight of something saved.

What does Jarvis think about now? After high school we went to different universities and saw each other just once or twice a year when our families got together for a Christmas drink or a long weekend barbeque. He had a lot of girlfriends, even brought some with him on weekends, but these visits did not coincide with mine. Then his parents moved to BC and I haven't seen him since. Last I heard, he went to the States, following the big money. I still hear bits and pieces of him from my mother, who talks with his mother on the phone, but she doesn't ask the questions I would ask, and so there are no clear answers.

I'd like to get Jarvis alone on a school bus again. I'd beckon him close and whisper, *the story goes like this.* Would he listen? Would he recognize the words?

Forest and rock, forest and rock all around. The neon sign in front of the bar has been turned off for over an hour, but a few people linger long past closing. The talk, low and disjointed, is of journeys made or yet to be made to places beyond the narrow streets and miles of trees. There is talk of dreams. The room is dim, made even dimmer by a haze of sweet-smelling smoke. A young man cups a harmonica to his mouth and plays an awkward tune of his own devising. He is thin and stringy, the muscles in his arms visible as they move against the bones beneath them. The woman wears a shirt that is loose and gauzy, no

"N. Loves Peggy"

bra, some beads. In the back pocket of her jeans she carries a small
notepad to jot down the words she wants to keep. She is fascinated
by the way he tongues the instrument, flutters his hand over it like a
single-winged bird. Each note travels her body's surface before settling
low in her belly. The weight of the music makes her move slowly as she
gets up, goes to sit cross-legged next to him. She reaches out, lays a
hand on him. The touch is like electricity. A jolt. Poetry. "Transformer
man," she whispers and he does not forget that phrase.

I want to hear Jarvis say, *yes, yes, that's how I remember it too.*

Sunday

TAMMY ARMSTRONG

ARMS OUTSTRETCHED, Little Sister spun in circles over the snow-drifted yard. My hand-me-down dress twisted around her thighs, tangling in the too-large jeans she'd pulled on beneath. Down on Brewer's Lane earlier, we'd dug up some softened acorns from below the snow around the oak trees. I'd stolen a jackknife from the top drawer of Father's bureau and was now popping the heads off each nut, making a neat incision down through the rotting iris then scooping out the meat. We kept the meat in an old kipper tin, unsure if it could be used for anything. We'd been told that everything could be used for something.

Little Sister's boots crunched over the snow as she spun. We were free now of the morning's sermon — the cracks and moans of the straight-backed pews; pews where we sat dangling our feet, enjoying the dark slushy puddles of dirt and snow beneath us. We'd practised balancing the collection quarters on our tongues through the hymns, knowing that when they fell to the lemon-polished floor, no one would be able to hear, over the high-pitched fervour of the choir, the infinite spin of the only money we'd be given all week. Mother never knew we sometimes tested God by spending the collection quarters on Monday. She never thought to ask where our sugar cravings came from. Cutting down too deep into an acorn, I threw the rotting thing into the snowdrifts. It sunk deep into a black-eyed air hole.

Sunday

We were to stay outside until lunchtime. Still mid-morning, the sun was spread too thin across the winter sky — the bay wind cold. I took my mittens off, placed my damp hands over my burning face, and looked from the verandah, out across the vastness of water. There was no movement. On warmer days, I'd seen the small heads of seals poke out through the shattered carpet of brash that moved into the Atlantic. There was nothing this Sunday except the pale blue and grey of torpid water — like Mother's chipped collection of Wedgwood. We would have at least three more months of winter.

I'd always looked forward to the first of April, for the break-up to begin. By Easter the sun would be strong, the thin pan of ice would sink and crash over itself throughout the day. We'd go down to the docks then with large hackmatack branches and push off the chunks that were shored by the current — everything pushed out to the coast of Maine. But it was still too soon.

Little Sister quit spinning. She lifted up the bunchy sleeve of her ski jacket and examined a scab that ran down the ridge of her elbow. Rug burn. I'd given it to her the day before. We'd been taking turns dragging each other over the copper shag in the rec room while Mother spoke on the phone about the neighbour. *Trudy's husband,* she'd hissed into the receiver. And Little Sister and I had dragged each other closer to the stool where she sat with the telephone balanced in the crook of her neck. *Cancer, I heard.* We knew what she was talking about: the gunshot that had rung out over the horseshoe-shaped road where we lived. It'd come from near the tiny cottages the older couples had win-terized years before, when no one dared live this close to the Bay of Fundy all year. There were too many weather warnings, too many times the Mounties had shown up to caution us about tail ends of hurricanes from Florida, too many winter storms that could have sunk the saltboxes we'd been trying to build. *He'd been just full of it. Nothing they could do.*

Friday, the afternoon of the shot, the storm had been bad.
We'd had to move from back to front of the bus all the way
home. School had been cancelled at lunch but it'd taken us nearly two hours to crawl from the Old Bay Road to Oak Bay. Our
abandoned lunch boxes and packs added ballast as they slid over
the icy rubber floors while we ran to the back windows to watch
the tires spin and chew into the barely sanded roads. We'd
thought it a game — thirty children, all content to clamber from
seat to seat. We'd giggled into our mitts, pulled staticy hats from
heads as the bus slowly crawled over the rugged ridges of southern New Brunswick. You could see the world from those ridges, I
thought. The farmland was clear some fifty miles away, revealing
logging roads like stretch marks through the hills and the St.
Croix River shinning along the coast. We imagined ourselves
elsewhere. On the other side.

The gunshot had happened just as we'd gotten off the school
bus. We'd looked up into the hoary sky, almost expecting a bevy
of quail — dark shadows against the day — but there was nothing. Hunting season had been over for some months. Ignoring the
shot, we'd crossed over the nearly plowed road onto the path
behind the Lowrey's house. We'd walked in thigh-deep snow,
balancing where the crust held until we arrived in our own yard,
stomped the caps of snow from our boot toes and punched our
thighs back into circulation. We forgot about the shot.

Couldn't bear to have the old soul look after him. Rug-burnt and
giddy, I'd pulled Little Sister almost to Mother's crocheted, slip-
pered foot. She'd waved her hands, shooing us out of the room,
jumping up at the same time to stir the chowder that bubbled
over the pot on the stove. *Poor old soul,* we'd heard Mother say
again before the pots and pans rattled out over her voice.

Little Sister crunched now over the path that led to the woodpile
and oil drum where last year's Sears catalogue and the receipts

Father didn't want Mother to find were burned. The path was covered in wood-stove ashes, to keep Father, if he happened to be around, from slipping with too many sticks of wood in his arms, with too much liquor snaking through his blood. She followed the soot path to the back of the house. From the road the house was white siding with red trim around the windows. But from the back, it was still tarpaper and flake board. The summer before, we'd discovered that clay from the backhoe treads could be used for drawing. We'd spent the day etching over the tarpaper, writing poems that Mother said little girls shouldn't be able to think up. The muddy streaks and words were still visible where the icicles and snow from the roof hadn't washed them away.

Little Sister walked until she was straight below the clothesline. She daintily lifted her dress and plunked herself down into tire tracks. Over the tracks she squirmed herself into a snow angel, leaving no evidence of her presence besides the two ski-boot prints at the bottom of the celestial skirt. She stood back to admire her work; it looked like a run-over angel. *Just like in church*, she said. Unsure how she meant it, I nodded in agreement.

This Sunday morning, it'd been quieter than usual while we got ready for church. Usually Father had been drinking for some hours and he'd insist on driving us up over the two hills himself. He'd sit in the driveway then until the service was over. On those kinds of mornings, his Merle Haggard eight-tracks would croon out trucking and prison songs for the elderly congregation in their shiny shoes, who knew Father as so-and-so's-gone-to-shit son. We knew that they mumbled to each other about us as they wrapped their Sunday coats closer to their pinched necks. Father would nod from the truck cab, drink his Ten Penny Tallboys and rant at whoever cared to listen about the uselessness of praying to some goddamn asshole.

On those mornings, Little Sister and I would beg Mother's

nerves to get better so she could sit with us. But she'd only shake her head, light another Matinee and send us away, each with a quarter in one mitt and a wad of tissue in the other. She hadn't come back to church since one morning several months before when she'd been playing with her tiny beaded change purse. She'd opened and closed the two-pronged latch until the coins slipped out onto the floor. We'd all chewed our fingernails down too far to pick up the coins, so she'd quickly torn off pieces of a matchbook, handing us each a strip. The three of us, on our hands and knees, flipped the coins up as the congregation again stood for "Lord of the Dance." Mother wouldn't come back after that, after she'd shuffled-squat among the zippered overshoes and ski boots. She never went back to that ten-pew church again.

Father must have had other things to do this morning. As we were heading into the house for lunch, he pulled up in the driveway. *Let's go to town,* he said. Little Sister and I hesitated near the oil barrel, then thought there might be a blackmail treat in there somewhere for us. We crawled up onto the cold vinyl seat, saying nothing as we bumped up the road towards town, as we passed Trudy's unplowed yard.

Trudy's husband had shot himself on Friday, with a twelve-gauge out behind their tiny house. I remembered years before, they'd had a large German shepherd tied on a chain out there. It'd kept us awake some nights in the summer with its barking and howling and the sadness of an impossible life — all wrapped around three feet of chain. Trudy's husband shot himself just after lunch. Biscuits and tomato soup. He would have tramped through the snow in those familiar dark green work pants and mackinaw, tramped through the woods until his wife wouldn't have been able to see him from the kitchen window, if she'd been standing there doing up the few saucers and utensils they'd used. He'd owned the property for several acres back, never developed though, had maybe enjoyed the expanse of space throughout the winter — ash trees like spent match heads along the perimeter, like veins in the spring. *Terminal.* He would have stood out there with the sky spitting down freezing rain. Pulling off the mittens that Trudy had made for him the year before, he'd placed them beneath his knees to keep away the ache as he knelt into the snow and positioned the shotgun at just the right angle. *Terminal.* He might have dug the butt down into the snow or maybe piled up a small knoll to keep it even with his head. *Terminal,* the doctor hadn't been able to say it enough. But there behind their small cottage with the yellow gingham curtains her husband remembered Trudy sewing before her eyes had gone bad, he would have placed the barrel in his mouth and tried to imagine his cells breaking apart, splitting into jagged bits of gristle.

There would have been only a moment of noise. Then the quiet, the hush of ice particles as they skimmed over the crusty field of snow, jingling softly like too many dimes in one pocket.

In the truck, Father lit his cigarettes with splintery Redbird matches. He tweezed them between his fingers, seeing something in the eye of each flame that only Lamb's Navy Rum would allow. I counted beneath my breath how long it took before the flame bit down onto the callused tip of his finger. One potato, two potato, three potato, four ... He tossed it out the window — his breath sour in the cold as he exhaled.

We were at the border, waiting to come back into Canada after being over to the American beer-and-wine store — always so bright and welcoming on Sundays. The customs officer frowned as he glanced quickly into the driver's window from his well-heated booth. He waved us through with his fingers. Smugglers now, Little Sister and I sat on a case of beer — an army blanket draped over it and our legs, made us look taller than our eight- and nine-year-old frames could possibly be. Our chests itched from the packs of cigarettes he'd wedged beneath our wool sweaters.

He dropped us off on the highway near Trudy's now-empty place. *Got someone to see*, he said as we jumped down from the cab. *Tell your mother, home later.* We fished the cigarettes from our clothes, tossed them onto the floor amidst the cassette tapes, tire gauge, and booster cables. He reached over, slammed the door and spun away. We stood there, listening to the wind churn up the first layer of snow on the fields, watching his tail lights until they blurred into a slanted red eye. Little Sister raised one mittened hand, palm towards her and I knew she'd given him the finger again.

I think Trudy's husband would have made sure to eat all of the biscuits in the basket. He would have quietly spread each mouthful with butter, using the bottom piece of the last biscuit to sop up the last of the tomato soup, wishing it had been peppered, and full of cheddar cheese, but probably content nonetheless. I imagine him cleaning up all the soup with that biscuit, until the biscuit was pink and the bowl revealed the small wisteria print at the bottom. He would have decided to tell her he was going out to bring in more wood. *More wood*, he'd say because she'd only nod then, focusing on the knitting she was trying to finish through her pearly cataracts. She wanted to finish the scarves for a craft sale, something their daughter organized each year. He couldn't be sure. Up near Mactaquac, he remembered. Somewhere near the dam, up that way. And he thought then about his daughter driving up the Trans-Canada with a cardboard box in the back seat full of his wife's winter scarves. He imagined her squinting, nose almost to the windshield as she tried to see through the snowstorms. It probably made him very sad. With the last of the soup gone, he would have poured some water into the bowl to make it easy to wash later. Then he would have turned to his wife who was already rummaging through the Save-Easy bag she used for holding knitting yarn. He would have turned to her then and said softly, *better get some more wood.*

We walked along the highway, peering into the sheet of weather for headlights, until we came to the darkened windows of Trudy's house. *Out back,* I said to Little Sister, unsure of my voice, of our direction once I said it. She kicked at the edge of the road for several seconds, gazing off across the field behind the house. We thought it could be back there — something we weren't allowed to know, to touch without consequences. We'd stood this way before, over freshly killed porcupines and dogs, close to the door frames when Mother and Father accused each other of dirty things. Something was different here. Little Sister walked around the mailbox, sinking and struggling in the ditch slush as she pulled herself back onto the road beside me. There were crows in the trees, laughing, bitching around us as we waited. Little Sister sighed and shook her head — the moment over, neither of us had the energy to double-dare, to go out alone behind the house.

Instead, we peeled open the metal mailbox that bent haphazardly at the side of the road. Along with all of our boxes, it'd been nicked too many times by the snowplow — the two-by-four scarred and chipped near the height of our knees. The lip was frozen shut. I spat then on the handle, breathing quickly until the metal loosened. We peered silently into the small, paper-cramped space for some time before I closed the door again. We headed back towards our house, through the darkening afternoon, through the fields that worked as baseball diamonds in the summer.

Mother stood on the verandah in those granny-square slippers and too-tight jeans. There were flour prints on her back pockets — Sunday was bread day. She stood on the verandah yelling above the diesel growl of our truck to where Father sat hunched over the wheel; a large woman in too-thick glasses sat close to him in the cab. I knew that she must have been straddling the stick shift, her feet probably resting on the cold tin of Father's lunch box. *Driving bitch,* Mother called it. *Goddamn asshole driving bitch 'round town for the world to see.* Little Sister kicked at the chains around a tire, then headed up the steps. Her toque was so far down over her eyes now that she had to lift her head up towards the sky to see her feet. I knew that ice was caking onto the bottom of Mother's slippers where she stood. I'd tested this myself earlier that winter, had stood in one spot until I couldn't stand it, amazed at how quickly the tiny balls of cold gathered beneath the curl of toes, the arch of foot.

We'd seen Father do this before — these new women with too-large teeth, from rundown shacks out near Pocalogan. *The sun always shines in Pocalogan,* Father would say when he was relaxed and had work. Little Sister and I stomped past our parents and the woman. We paused on the porch — damp mittens squeaking between our teeth as we dusted off the acorn pipes from beneath new snow. We left the kipper tin there.

On the braided rug near the wood stove, Little Sister and I sat stretched with moccasin toes touching. Each with an acorn pipe in our mouth, we peeled open Trudy and her husband's letters — the glue frozen, then damp, pulled away from our fingers easily. We kept categories in an ellipse around our shivering bodies: Christmas cards, sorry cards, the letters with too-tiny writing on pale blue paper. We kept the shopping flyers for last — satisfied with the coloured photos — the brightness that told us all we really needed to know.

Assumptions

LIZA POTVIN

MY FATHER WAS descended from a Pepsi, or a rotten-tooth, as the lowlife francophones like my grandfather were called in Belle Rivière. In the twilit hours of humid Ontario evenings, you can still see these shackers sitting on the wide stoops of their decrepit tarpaper houses, drinking ale and flinging bottles onto the porch. Most sported sweat-grimed undershirts stretched tautly over what they proudly referred to as "Molson's muscles." In their teens and early twenties, they wore tight trousers and strutted down the streets or drove fast cars; they believed they were big time operators, smooth and immortal, intact.

The lucky ones had jobs in nearby Tecumseh or a half-hour's drive across the bridge in Flint, working in the auto plants and making decent money, which they squandered on enormous RCAs and Chevrolets. Those who were not blessed with good luck spoke to their wives and children through bars. And no Pepsi could gain the respect of the Anglos until he could afford a month in Florida every winter; a Miami tan was worn like a badge in southern Ontario, where the last thing anyone wanted was camouflage.

The youngest boy from a family of twenty-two, my father would feel each sweltering supper hour melt into early evening. As summer took over, he watched the acrid sun sink into the steam of nightfall. He sat on the stoop alongside his siblings and garrulous neighbours, and listened to gossip, as he turned his head first to face one person on his left side and then to another on his right side. It never really cooled down enough to sleep at night for more than a few hours.

When he realized that this sideways glancing would get him nowhere, my father turned his gaze upwards instead. Whether it was from a quickness of mind, impatience, or both, he recognized that flying away was more expedient than running away. My father was noted in school as an ace with numbers who painted model airplanes and had serious thoughts about the sky and the planets. He was only seventeen when he joined the Royal Canadian Air Force. Given full gold wings, he wore the RCAF insignia imprinted on the centre of the crest on his shoulder, where it divided into rich black and red embroidered patterns. He was also given a language of precision, designed to say every-thing necessary for the rebuilding of post-war empires, a brown leather jacket, and a ready-made self-regard.

He cruised at high altitudes in his Lancaster Mark II. Yet none of these things could ever mask my father's lifelong sense of infe-riority: a French-Canadian stationed in France, whose accent was never pure enough, whose unerasable *joual* earned him as much teasing in the bistros there as it did in the taverns of English Canada. My father never got to see combat, so he invented his own. And thus we became a part of his personal war.

We were living in the barracks near Metz one grey French winter, and my father was trying to decide where we should go for a brief spring holiday. "'Bout time I got some goddamn R 'n' R," he said, slurring his words. My mother wanted to go somewhere warm. But her suggestions for possible holiday destinations were shot down immediately, and she put up no struggle. My father's Air Force buddy, Karl, had been the one to suggest going for mus-sels in Brussels. The two of them were sitting at the kitchen table late one night, drinking and smoking, and snatches of their loud conversation drifted up the stairs as I was falling asleep. I was

Assumptions

nine years old, but accustomed to my father's drinking binges. Most nights when my father drank in the kitchen, he sank into one of his accusatory moods, and we could hear him yelling at my mother, dark and horrible noises that filled the barracks and spilled over into our dreams. I was the eldest, and he hated me the most for not being a son he could be proud of. When he remembered that my mother had forgotten to give him a boy yet, he would turn to me in slow recognition of my face and spit in it with the slow calmness of the alcoholic whose gestures become nearly graceful by habit.

But on this night he was excited, full of plans, "*Bebert*, keep your voice *down*," my mother kept interjecting, but to no avail. My father had prepared one of his favourite dishes for supper, rabbit stew. Years later my middle sister, Odette, revealed, with a shudder in her voice, what his cooking secret was: he bled the freshly killed hare's blood from its neck directly into the stewing pot. Now I am not so certain I would relish the taste of the stew as much as I used to. I no longer want my portion of such dishes, but certain smells alone can take me back to that day. The slow-cooking aroma had filled our tiny officer's quarters for days, and that night I had taken great pleasure in ladling the rich stew over my spaghetti, removing the delicate bones after my teeth found them. Karl's boisterous appreciation and numerous bottles of local red wine increased my father's delight. The two of them began talking food, which led to memory, which led to travel and the scheme of driving to Brussels two weeks later to eat mussels. It was not until many years later the phrase "mussels in Brussels" would acquire a wistfulness, become a family anecdote, a litany of better times.

We were all duly packed into the rusty Citröen: three girls cramped into the back, our legs perched on top of the suitcases, our immobility making it easier to pinch one another. "I'm going to give you what you deserve if you don't sit still," my father threatened. "But she's asking for it," my youngest sister,

Francine, responded, and I dug my nail harder into her thigh to make her be quiet. "That's it! I've had enough!" he would explode. "Everybody out for some fresh air!" We would run before he caught us and vented his anger. Usually this involved his removing his Air Force belt and bending us across his knee until our bottoms were so sore we could not sit without weeping. But he also made it clear that he would not put up with such weaknesses as tears, so we learned not to whimper after he strapped us. We pretended to be entranced by the wildflowers across the field where we stopped, and flew off to gather a bouquet for our mother. The drive took the better part of the first day, but we made many stops to sniff out bakeries which sold Easter breads, then ate and slept at a small family hotel. It was drizzling a bit as we approached Brussels early the next morning, settled into our *pension*, unloaded all the bottles my father had consumed in the car into the trash bin, and got ready to go out.

Mostly I remember that day as the first occasion to wear my shiny new patent leather shoes. Every spring my father handed my mother money to buy us girls new shoes. He was insistent that we should have the best leather. His own feet were badly deformed and he suffered from hammer toes, a condition made worse by his being the last in line for hand-me-down shoes. I have maintained, although often been unable to afford, a taste for elegant leather shoes. I was wearing my new Easter shoes for the first time that April when we climbed up three sets of stairs to arrive at the restaurant Karl had recommended to my father. I also had on new white knee socks that offset the black patent leather in a very pleasing way, I thought, as I clicked my heels together in what my dance teacher called *plier*, almost as if my shoes had wings.

I could see my face in my shoes all the way up the stairs, they shone so much! My father poked his finger into my backside from the step below me, too hard, until I winced in pain. "Hurry

Assumptions

up! You're as bad as your mother," he said. On the very top
floor, in a small room, we were seated at a table with a red and
white gingham cloth. My mother, who was wearing a green suit
she had made herself after seeing a similar ensemble worn by
Jackie Kennedy in a fashion magazine, reminded us to remember
our manners. "Especially you. And don't wipe your snotty nose
on the napkin," my father snarled at me. I could smell the stale
wine fumes on his breath from all the way across the table. My
mother folded her own cloth napkin neatly in her lap and passed
the breadbasket to my father.

And then the mussels began to arrive, plateful after steaming
plateful, platters of mussels smothered in tomato sauce, others in
garlic and butter, some marinated in wine and herbs. The smell
in the air was heavenly, all yeasty warm from the bread, and
fresh sautéed garlic teased my nose, but I could tell from my
father's stern glance that this was one of his moments of glory,
not to be interrupted by my enthusiastic comments under any
circumstances. And I knew well enough not to touch the food
until he had helped himself first. "Children need to be seen and
not heard," my mother's echoing of his admonition seemed to
ring in my ears. Before we were allowed to dig into them, my
father made us fold our hands: *"Seigneur, nous vous prions ..."* He
had already had too much wine and his face was overly ruddy
for this early hour. Yet I had never expected that he would make
us say grace or that he might expose our family prayer rituals so
publicly. He expected us to feel beholden to him, to remember
that these were the very best mussels, that May would bring the
smaller Danish mussels, that we were here just in time.

I am not sure why I felt so mortified since it was a Catholic
city and the waitress and other patrons never took any notice of
us. I believe my father wanted our everlasting gratitude for his
bounty when he spread his hands and said, "Let us have grace."
I gripped my fingers tightly against the backs of my hands and
lowered my head in prayer, but again, all I could smell and

32

breathe and think was garlic.

Suddenly he noticed me beside him, turned his head to look below the table, and said, "What are you wearing those ridiculous stockings for? They make your knees look like fat sausages." I wilted. Suddenly my new shoes seemed tawdry, and my pretension of patent-leather glamour, a sham. My stomach churned as it usually did when he made comments about my ugliness. For thirty years thereafter I believed I was ugly, and made it a habit not to look in mirrors. I caught my mother's glance briefly before she turned to watch the waiter moving towards the table with more food. I had learned long ago that my mother always took his side, and always did exactly as he said. She was beautiful in that quiet moment, her head downcast, in spite of the marks he had left across her cheek the night before, and I secretly believed that I resembled her just a little.

I prayed until I finally found something I could be grateful to God about: at least we were in a restaurant, and chances were that I wouldn't get the usual whack across the back of my head that accompanied my father's displeasure with me. In public he was the model father. All I could do was make the sign of the cross against my forehead, lips, and chest, and ask God why I had to have a father who could be so mean to all of us in one moment, and so generous in the next. I was learning from experience that not everything that is incredible is untrue.

Pewter-coloured buckets filled with French fries arrived at his elbows, and we set to the meal. But I cannot really remember what the mussels tasted like. I was too distraught and angry with God for being unfair. I do remember that it was the first time I didn't have to drink my wine watered down, only because in his distraction my father forgot. And that, after a crisp green salad, another accompaniment arrived at our table: the first white asparagus spears of spring, wrapped in wilted leaks tied into bows, drizzled with butter, parsley, and pepper, and served on a red platter. It was the prettiest dish on the table. Biting one of those white asparagus tips, I thought I had never tasted any vegetable so divine, a texture at once luxurious and simple. In all of my culinary quests since, there has never been any comparison. If I have any taste today, if my hunger is inspired and rampant, I attribute it to the taste of white asparagus.

Later that afternoon we toured Brussels. It is a city whose palaces, museums, and basilicas have a rich Gothic texture. But for me the former guild houses in the *Broodhuis* inspired a certain chill. Perhaps my career as an art critic began at the moment I saw the holy card, which had baroque warmth that the city itself did not possess. Mostly because I still have a postcard of it, I also remember all too clearly the famous statue of the little pissing boy, called the *Mannekin-Pis*, who is supposed to have extinguished by "watering" a firecracker meant to blow up the Town-Hall. Other legends had it that he was the son of a rich bourgeois, found by his grateful parents at the corner of the rue l'Étuve and the rue du Chene, relieving himself in the same manner as the famous fountain. It has become a symbol of all the city's tragedies and fortunes. I think of it when I recall the grubby street urchins who played on the paving stones outside the church, wondering if their parents would have even sent out a search party should news of their children's disappearance be made known. I think of the miracle of the fountain's survival, its mocking and arrogant arc of water spouting into the air, when I sift through the sepia-toned photographs of rubble-strewn postwar cities.

But it was really the holy card that captured my most intense memory of Brussels. We went to church early that evening. I collected holy cards for my missal from every church I visited with my parents. Some of these I traded with other girls from my catechism class. For many years of Sundays, I remained enamoured of the gilded picture I bought with my allowance at the gift shop at St. Catherine's in Brussels, a fourteenth-century church rebuilt in 1850. It was a version of the Assumption that I eventually learned is attributed to that "meticulous Flemish realist" who alone succeeded in "unifying myth and reality": Rubens. I remember being astounded by the pull between heaven and earth, the voluptuous virgin, the brilliant darkness, so much muscular light and glory.

On the back of the card was written mysteriously: *Expleto terres tris pitae cursu.* My fifth-grade Latin teacher, a Jesuit, later translated it for me as: "The Immaculate Mother of God, the ever-Virgin Mary, having completed the course of her earthly life, was assumed body and soul into heavenly glory." (Much too lugubrious. I have always preferred the compactness of Latin.) He went on to explain the official Church doctrine on Mary's privileged role as daughter, spouse, and mother; as Adam's love for Eve led him into sin, so Christ's love for Mary led Him to allow her to share in the conflict. This escaped me entirely, and made me sorry I had asked. My favourite features of the holy card were the rays of gold emanating from Mary's soaring arms as she rose towards heaven. I returned my eyes again and again to the Rubens and was swept up into the unending light.

My parents must also have loved the blinding white light because they became snowbirds and settled in Florida when my father retired, where they assumed that the sun would keep them eternally young. My father also assumed that happiness was something that could be bought or achieved if he just found the magic formula; he never learned that happiness is not a permanent condition but a relative state, a matter of degree. I have had my share of assumptions too. For one thing, I always assumed that I too could fly. Indeed in my dreams I flew all the time, and had difficulty accepting the reality that, if I stood on the edge of some cliff, I should not be able to take off with the same ease I did in those dreams. I assumed I would always be as ugly as my father informed me I was, and did not assume I had the right to be beautiful. I had also assumed that my lifelong argument with God about what was fair and what was not, begun that spring in

Assumptions

Brussels, would go on forever and forever, and I had planned on winning. I had not assumed that I would be left here, standing alone, shouting in the dark.

My father committed suicide last Tuesday night. My youngest sister, Francine, who had stayed in touch with my parents many years longer than I cared to, called to tell me the news, and to ask whether or not I wanted to attend the funeral. I had not spoken to my father in eight years, not since he had rearranged the fine bones of my mother's face beyond recognition, the year before they retired to Florida. I tried to picture her again, smiling in the Jackie Kennedy suit, how proud she had been of it, but all I could think of was her bandaged head in the hospital, how even her tears couldn't escape the eye slits carved in the plaster covering her mummified face. My sister announced that my parents had been reading *Romeo and Juliet* the week before their deaths, that my mother had called to tell her that she was newly enamoured of Shakespeare. I cannot envision what demons my father grappled with as he lay in that white room in a Miami condo, curled up in a fetal position, nor can I guess what memories haunted him as he clutched the same weapon he had used to kill my mother several hours earlier. Perhaps he cried afterwards, not for her, but for himself. Human beings are rarely given to understand what occurs between them in the darkness. Most of us recover by mourning; others encounter only the madness. Let us have grace, then.

My father still stands in my mind, young, dignified and handsome, raised halfway up the staircase that leads to a small restaurant in Brussels. He is wearing his RCAF uniform, the distressed leather jacket covering his wings, its brown softness and fine fissures gleaming in the light from the open window on the landing. It is a weak spring light, but gentle somehow, barely illuminating his face and changing his otherwise invisible eyelashes into a startling haloed fringe around eyes that are sad and hungry; I am condemned to see those eyes every morning in my mirror. I do look at myself in the mirror now, and I know that I am not ugly. But when I look carefully at the scene in Brussels, I see that he stands there, poised in flight, one leg up on the next stair, bent over so that he can extend one arm towards me as I climb upwards, beckoning. The staircase below is only dimly lit, and outside the sun is descending slowly over the evening. It is an indeterminate season; the ground is still damp with winter's cold breath but musty with the warmer odours of packed dirt, stale beer, urine. Fog swirls around the building, the streets are paved with sombre concrete and cracked cobblestones, the vendors are closing their stalls now, and the ghosts of incomplete conversations linger in empty alleyways.

Looking down upon that edifice, the first thing I notice is that the roof is flat, but as I rise higher and higher, that it is surrounded by a certain lustre. Drawing back, pulling away, my hand on the throttle of the engine of a Lancaster Mark II bomber, I stare down upon the tiny city of Brussels in the expanding dark night. The smaller it grows in the distance, the greater my compulsion to recall the erosion of an embattled Europe. Others could be forgiven if they believed that all that could be seen in that evolving twilight beneath them was one city twinkling its neon-lit eyes at them, or if it appeared to them that thousands of tiny white votive tapers were being lit to usher in the blackening night. But I know, God knows, and my father knows, that these are young, tender, white asparagus shoots. And they are everywhere, luminous, just below the surface of the earth, reaching towards the sky.

Carmen: The Idea of Red

MELANIE LITTLE

TWO THINGS

THAT'S IT, all there is to know about you. One: You are in grade
six. Two: You have this leg, your left, exactly four inches longer
than your right. One + Two is not a happy equation.

Each night, in pursuit of parity, you tie your big right toe to
your bed-canopy rail with the aid of an unloved octopus made of
purple yarn. Then you move your right hip as far up towards the
pillow as it will go. You try to conjure dreams of being pulled
apart —

>   cell by cell by cell,
>   like a never-snapping
>   rubber band.

But it's only the left leg that ever hurts. And it does, continually, and a lot.

You're seeing a physiotherapist, a man with powder blue
shirts and an office above the Ford dealership. He makes you lie
on a big red inflatable ball, tells you to lift one leg and then the
other. You try to steady yourself, your curled toes clawing at the
floor, but the ball always body-flips you before you can do it

twice. The therapist strides around the room, working the floor like a talk-show host, calling out encouragement: cementing patients to each other across beds, barbells, balls, all manner of injuries. "Pretend you're in a lake," he yells over to you one day from where he's applying karate chops to the back of a construction worker named Fred. "You're floating on your back, swimming." And the red ball wobbles beneath you, finds its centre, and is still.

MOON ROCKS

Even this far north, the snow is spiked, peppered with stones. You know because they hold you down in it, rub your face in the sharp sidewalk mess. You buck up, rearing, and icicles sprout from your nostrils in the minus-forty-degree air. If you come home looking like this, with the frozen snot still trailing under your nose, your mom will tell you you are a walrus, and sing —
koo-kook — achoo!
But your mom sometimes says: This is the hardest place on earth. Before you were born, the American astronauts came up here to practise walking on the moon.
The rock gets into everything. Patches of it jump up from the snow like the spiky, tufty-bald heads of hatchling birds. You imagine the Americans shuffling along the rock in their Michelin-Man space suits; they bang the ends of their flagpoles over and over against the ground, swearing in their twangy accents, trying to find a soft spot.

IGOR

In school, you hide: anywhere you can. Behind the stage curtain at lunch. At recess, because you are forced to go outside, beneath the sissy slide no one past kindergarten will acknowledge. In the cloakroom, until the last possible minute, before the start of class.

From there, you watch. *Mork & Mindy* T-shirts give chase through the schoolyard, screech *Nanoo! Nanoo!* in time to their attacks. Boys' hands turned scissors between the corduroy legs of —

You! Girls! What's going on there?

You learn that adults always catch the wrong thing, turn the wrong cheek, zoom in on the ones made dumb by innocence.

They call you Igor, after the hunchbacked, drooling servant on *The Hilarious House of Frankenstein*. It isn't fair, no one said it was fair: you have only a limp, not a hump. But you don't protest. You never tell anyone outside the school — your mother, for instance. You don't dare say the word "Igor" out loud, afraid to give it that much credence. The speaking of it might cement it to you forever, might engrave it upon the air you breathe.

In your dreams, though, the leg takes on a life of its own, and it is named Igor. In the dreams it follows you everywhere, chattering like a well-meaning but humiliating (snot-nosed maybe, or stinky) best friend. But Igor is never you. It is only the leg.

Perhaps in revenge, you name your succession of cats after other monsters on *House of Frankenstein*: Griselda, Swami, Wolfman Jack. You dress them up in outfits you make from your own discarded clothes and you give them corresponding fur-dos with manicure scissors. Sometimes you nick the skin. The cats never stick around for long.

CARMEN AND THE JOLLY CREW

They are always laughing. The kids at your school are laughing all the time. Your mother went there once, to talk to your gym teacher about your *limitations*. "They're quite the jolly crew, aren't they?" she said.

The boys get down on bended knee

for Carmen
crooning like gulls
I loooove you

Jeaned knees grind on ice and asphalt, grovel in laughter's giddy thrall. Homage to Carmen, who smells of earth; Carmen, who (they say) smells of shit. Flowers picked from the weedy school garden, ironic offerings pinned and flattened under the feet of their laughter. Boys made brave by boots named for big wild animals and gym bags which sing-sign All Day I Dream About Sex. Leather handles curve-carved, brittle as bone, cracking in the wind-chill factor like the tight-made up smiles of your teachers.

Whenever Carmen comes into view the boys come running, serenading her Speedy Gonzales-style with their scorn —

Andale, andale, eeepa eeepa, ya! ya! ya!

Their call snakes around your insides, around the moments of your day like an echo, an infectious refrain.

No one knows why she is here. She was just there, in class, in the yard, in the auditorium, on the first day of grade six. There were no announcements by the teachers or over the P.A.

People know only two things about Carmen. One: She speaks Spanish. Two: She speaks English too, knows more words than most of the kids at school, but pronounces them with what is widely felt to be a Dracula accent. One + Two is not a happy equation.

But you know other things.

She has a gold tooth.

Also: wide hips, swathed in black gabardine. Wears them with an orange-and-white striped shirt, breasts, a womanly smell that goes

sometimes sour after softball

You write those four words in the back of your geometry book. Alliteration, a word which sounds like it's about garbage. You decide to like that about it, as well as its assault on the corners of things.

Those black pants have silver zippers at different angles all down the fronts of the legs. You'd like to give a precise count, but are afraid to look long enough.

But, you are always watching, and soon you know that altogether, there are ten.

COUTURE

"Your mother still dresses you," the kids accuse, and this is true, in a sense. Your mom is cursed, she says, with the impossible task of seeing that you look fit to leave the house.

She can't sew, a fact she is perversely proud of, but any and every store-bought pair of pants leave your left anklebones exposed as the Adam's apples of the older boys. "Where's the flood?" they yell.

So your clothes are hand-sewn, but by the other mothers. You go to their houses and stand in your underwear to be measured while their kids, your peers, snigger from the kitchens, storing ammunition for tomorrow. But your mother is never happy with the results of these visits, the single subject on which the two of you ever agree. By now you have a different outfit sewn by the mother of almost every kid in your class.

The day before Easter break, a big tyrant-girl named Bev calls Carmen over. "C'mere, Taco, I need ta tellya a secret." Carmen is getting acclimatized, so she hangs back, knows that much. You're standing right near, at your locker. "'Kay," says Bev, "be that way. Maybe I'll tell Igor instead. But's your goddamn loss." Carmen looks over at you, squinting through her pink-plastic cat's-eye glasses. She goes up to Bev. "Closer," says Bev. "We don't want Igor to hear. She's eavesdropping as usual." Carmen leans in.

Bev spits in her face, a bright blue splat because she's been sucking a Gobstopper, Berry Berry Blue. The rhinestones on the corner of Carmen's left lens disappear in a puddle of inky ooze. "Sorry," says Bev. "Don't know the Spanish translation."

You keep growing. By now you're stooping (from a distance) over all the boys, and most of the other girls (except Bev) in your class. Your leg grows with you.

More than ever, you need new clothes. The situation is Dire, says your mother, who loves that word. She is willing to give in, to concede to yet another round of condescending salesgirls and shoddy department-store alterations. She will pick you up after school.

Your mother picks you up but the car does not go in the direction of downtown. Instead, it pulls up in front of an apologetic-looking house in the south end, black paper with words on it for siding, one of those ones that get started, but never finished, like a science project that came due before the labels could be glued on. A high front door hovers in empty air, loopily free of the accompaniment of steps. You can imagine opening it and striding out into a freefall. "Well," says your mother. "I guess we'll use the side entrance."

Carmen's mother is the most gorgeous woman you've ever seen, except on TV. The front of her dress is cut into the shape of a Valentine's Day heart. Her nails are red, but they are a burnished, warm, chesterfield-red, not metallic or bloody like the nails of the girls at school. She invites you inside with a flourish.

Carmen doesn't smirk from the kitchen but instead sits on a cushion at your feet. If she notices you're in your underwear, she doesn't show it. She has a pen and paper and she writes down numbers as her mother calls out the elegy of your measurements in a plaintive, musical voice. In Spanish, the sound of you is almost beautiful. You stare into the bleeding porcelain heart of Jesus on the mantle and allow yourself to feel seduced. There is

also a poster you instantly love, a chart depicting fifty perfect
little squares of colour whose names you've never heard before —
magenta,

aubergine,

cyan.

Carmen's mother goes into another room and returns with a
long, shimmering skirt in velvet ripple. "Not to wear until
Christmastime, too much drama," she says. "But it will be free
for you — Carmen has got too fat."

The skirt whispers against your skin as Carmen helps her
mother pin it where it must be taken in. The pins emanate from
her mouth, point out, like the rays of the sun. "Beautiful girl,
now, yes?" her mother says.

You look from the skirt to the chart and back again. "What
colour is it?" you ask. Finally, Carmen laughs at you. But her
mother answers solemnly, as if she considers this a very good
question. "It is red," she says.

RED

You don't want to wait, you won't wait for Christmas, and when
you're home you run around in the skirt, swirling a dance in
front of your mother's big mirror, grabbing the hem at one side
and pretending it's a bullfighting cape.

"Why does red make them mad?" you ask your mom.

"Who gets mad?"

"You know, the bulls. It makes them charge."

"It's not the colour. It's the movement, I think."

"So why is the cape always red? Does it have to be?"

"Oh, I don't know. Give me a break, will you?"

You won't. "Can't we go look it up at the library?"

"Oh for fart's sake. It's just a symbol, okay? It's not the
colour, like I said. It's just the idea of it. Now take that thing off,

you look like an accident."

At night, you no longer dream of the leg. Instead there you are, in Carmen's black zippered pants and waving the red skirt like a flag. Your feet dance in the schoolyard —
                    crushing snow and stone
                                    like flesh and bone.
            You move to your own rhythm,   both legs
                            dancing amidst
            the searing flirt of bulls.

The real world: you've forgotten your English notebook at school. You know that whatever you leave in your desk overnight will be poppy-nail pilfered and snigger-screech broadcast by the time you lumber to school the next morning. Your journal is in that notebook. You're late for supper, hell will be paid, but you must go back.

The minute before you open the door to the English class-room the fact of presence hits you like a warm, wet cloth, but it's too late to stop the momentum of your legs (especially Igor, which has a mind of its own). You brace for a volley of insults, rocks, parodic kisses of spit. Instead all you see is a hand, and what it is doing. Carmen's boob is out and the nipple jumps and slides around obscenely between enormous, hairy fingers, stretching and receding like a little cartoon face on a glob of Silly Putty. You look up, then, and see Mr. Haines's face crashing in and out of Carmen's like he's eating it.

"I want to mine your mouth with my tongue," you hear him say.

When you remember this years later, you will believe you made it up.

THE FAST FRIENDS

Despite the language barrier, your mother and Carmen's mother have become fast friends. That's what yours always calls it when she's talking to other ladies — older, dubious friends of longer standing (does that make them slow friends? you wonder). It makes you picture the two of them speeding along in a car, laughing and holding hands like the women in this movie she took you to once. So when she announces that the four of you are going to drive to the cottage together, "Just us girls," you are afraid. You pull your seat-belt as tight as it will go and when you finally get to stop and stretch Igor out under the trees you see an angry red welt across the top of your chest. Carmen shakes her head, she's already not talking to you, she couldn't even be bothered to put her own seat-belt on. Her eyes seem to move back and forth behind her lowered, fed-up lids like they're writing down mental notes of your idiocies to use as trading cards when September comes again.

In the musty upper bunk of your cottage room you dream of Carmen. "I want your mouth as mine with my tongue," she says. When you wake up you look down and your left-foot toenails have all been painted black.

QUESTIONS

"Your country is stupid," she says. The two of you are lying on the island across the bay from your cottage, tanning. Right now the sun is beating down like a slap. The dried-out droppings from the fir trees needle painfully at your bare skin. Earlier that day you were in the water when it started to snow. It is the middle of June. You don't argue her point.

This island has been deserted for as long as you can remember. It's always had one abandoned shack, though, and when you were smaller that shack was the scene of all sorts of imagined plots, secret societies, sex crimes, and wild teenage orgies to which you were never invited. These last few years, you've forgotten all these phantasms in one gelatinous mass of neglect; the island has become just another speck on the lens of your mind's eye. Carmen makes you remember.

You play Truth or Dare. Carmen's questions are not like your cousins'; she doesn't just say, *Have you ever kissed a boy, Have you ever done it,* and so on, things to which your answers are always depressingly obvious before the questions are even asked. Carmen's questions are things like *Have you ever wished your mother harm* and *Have you ever put something alive in your mouth.* They make you want to change the subject, which is why you pick Dare next. Which is why you're lying there with your flat chest pressed directly against the itchy undergrowth, your clothes in a heap on the floor of the shack, equally abandoned.

Carmen is smoking, billowing out rings that look like the flattened Os of diced green onions. You have to say something, anything, to make her get away from you, to make her stop looking. I dare you to set it on fire, you say, backing towards the door.

Carmen licks her lips. "Yum," she says, a word you know she's copying from your mother. "Yum," your mom said, when Carmen's mom pulled a case of wine out of the trunk of the car last night.

For too long, Carmen doesn't come back out. It's cold again, and Igor is starting its little sing-song of pain in your head. Finally, you pick your body up and creep over to the broken window. Inside, your clothes are a black, burning heap on the table.

In the boat, for she is there already, she says, "Look," pointing, and you see that there is a black line of earth over your heart. Carmen puts her finger on it, blurs the edges sideways to make a capital I. Then she draws her finger away and you think she's going to brush something on herself too. You catch yourself wishing it. But she bends over the side and washes her hand in the lake.

Naked, you are moving towards your cottage. Or rather, you

are being moved. Carmen has the oars. The fire has spread to the rest of the shack now and the reflection of your skin glows white in Carmen's lenses. There is no hope of camouflage. You wonder what your mothers are doing at this moment. What will they see if they look? Will they look? And if they do, will the fire behind you make your bodies appear red, white, or some other colour whose name you don't yet know?

Wire Basket

GAÏTANE VILLENEUVE

ME AND LENNY. We imagine that city lights look like a falling sky. Hovering above the concrete, shooting stars through some fancy office window or out on some movie star's balcony. Big city lights making up a little sky. Here in Dally, on nights when they call the water civil — those nights when each resting wave has fallen into the other — the only lights to be seen are the straight beams of white that run north and south across the bay. Reflecting the boundaries. We don't believe lights could lie that flat surrounded by tall buildings.

We drive around town — the same street — up and down, listening to some seventies rhythm that stops our minds from drifting beyond the valley walls that surround us. There are no glowing signs showing when to start and when to stop, or neon symbols signalling Walk — Don't Walk. The music, like a metronome, keeps us on course. Brings us up to speed. Slows us down just this side of the faded stop sign that allows a driver time to think before exiting Dally.

Lenny says he wishes he was retarded. I begin to smile, but then I look at him. He's a little too big with jeans that fit a little too tight. His hair is too long, but it falls just right like one of those Dukes of Hazard boys. Lenny smells good. Like the way clothes smell when they're dried outside. Like freshly cut wood. I think that I would love him if I could. Lenny says he'd like to ride around town on a bicycle with a clothespin clipped to his left pant leg to keep it from getting caught in the naked, rusty chain. I try to remember which side of the bike the chain turns on, but I can't recall. Lenny says if he was retarded he wouldn't know how hard it is to find a job. He wouldn't worry about his rent being paid on time. He could just sit on his front porch and yell pleasantries and obscenities at the people who walk by.

I laugh. Lenny says he wouldn't think about what now consumes his mind in this small town. He says that the questions aren't what bother him. It's the answers that keep him up at night. He says that everyone would like him if he was retarded because no one dislikes retarded people. It isn't polite. They would all say "Poor Lenny," and mumble under their breaths about not knowing any better. They would all smile and take comfort in their assurances that God looks out for his flock when they join him in His kingdom. Being polite and righteous is very important in a small town, Lenny reminds me. I laugh again. Lenny tries to laugh too. I say that people like him now. Still, he thinks he would be happier with canvas shoes and a standard bike with a wire basket on the front.

One old song after another rises out of the radio and we fall into silence. I stare out my window. I don't need to focus. I see the same things every night. Two funeral parlours. Three seniors' rest homes. Deserted fish plant. Yellow light over the post office. Blue block letters on the brown brick town hall. The numbers on the clock change form. I'm inhaling Lenny's scent. Eleven o'clock and all is the same. Every night we drive and listen to the same songs. Melodies channelled along some distant live wire. Transmitting. Emitting. The chorus repeats. Our silence crescendos. Programmed by some man in a little room. Surrounded by big radio sound.

We drive up and down the same street and neither of us dares look past the valley. The dark green hills stand before us like guards. Keeping us out. Keeping us in. Balancing our horizon like some tightrope act. I glance over at Lenny and wonder how the truck stays on the road. He's staring out his side window the way he does every night. In his narrow-road habit. Leaning towards the door — face pressed against the glass. Watching the water closing in on it all.

Lenny turns the volume dial down and asks if I would sit with him on his porch if he was retarded. Most friends aren't by choice in a small town. I think to be emotional. I think to tell him that maybe I would take him more seriously if he was retarded. I think to tell him that he doesn't have a front porch. I think to tell him yes.

"Only if you let me ride your bike," I say and turn the volume up again.

I glance at the eight ball that's Krazy Glued to the top of the gear shift. Somewhere — outside of here — there are fourteen balls that are useless because we have the one that determines the game. In a dingy pool hall with hustlers and losers, the balls are racked. I'm ready to break. Send a triangle of constellations — striped and solid stars — hurling through some green sky.

I reach my hand into the soaked cardboard box that sits between us, take a handful of cold, greasy fries, and look out the window again.

"I have to show you something," Lenny says.

"What is it?" I ask.

Lenny says nothing.

We are going to leave the valley. We are going to follow the highway far from this town. Drive across and off this island. Where the songs of crickets echo in the dry autumn air. And the voices of strangers meld together in an impolite harmony. I sit up straight. Begin to lean forward. I want to count the city lights. From the tacky motel Vacancy signs to the lit high-rise eyes. I don't want to miss one light.

But we drive past the access to the highway. We head north again. Through my steamed side window I see everything I have seen in my life.

"There's nothing down here," I say.

"We're not there yet."

Lenny turns to look at me, but turns away and laughs uneasily. For just a moment I think that I would be afraid if I lived in a city or in one of those farming states where girls are found raped and murdered in some cornfield. There's always a story like that on the late-night news. The reporters say that she was a nice girl who smiled all the time. She had lots of friends and no one would ever want to harm her. She was a smart girl — knew not to put herself in danger. Honour roll. Girl next door. She could feel the rustling of leaves under her feet as she skipped along a forested path. She could breathe in the cold crisp mountain air. She could smell the salty seaside spray. Hear the ocean's voice call out from inside a pretty shell. She had dreams when he told her how they would leave those fields — leave the stretching land and go where hills cradled the roads. She was full of hope as he drove deeper and deeper into the harvested field.

We reach the dead end and Lenny turns the truck around. He pulls off and stops on the wrong side of the road. Because you can do that in a small town.

"Why are we stopping here?" I ask.

"Exactly," says Lenny.

"Why?" I ask again.

Looking past his pointed finger, I see the shape of the town lights. A long, distorted letter Y.

Lenny has his foot on the brake. We sit in his rusty pick-up truck, gazing at the Y as if we had discovered a new constellation. In front and to one side, but nothing shining above us. A universe. With the water closing in on it all. And we wait. For our time to leave. For something to change. We wait for someone to buy that sixty-something Mustang down the street. I tell Lenny it's been painted yellow. Lenny mumbles that it's a brush and roller job, and turns his head away. I talk about the boy next door who still lives next door and about how his wife is painting their front door a new colour this week. The magazines at the drug store say blue is in this season. The boy-next-door's wife isn't from here and doesn't understand why she is the only one painting.

I watch Lenny as he sits there, wrapped up in his silence. Examine him like a vulture waiting to strike her prey. Stare at his softness like a mother in wonder of what she has created. I reach out to touch him, but my hand only makes it to the cold, chewy fries.

Lenny watches the rock that sits in the middle of the bay. The rock of legends. That only the strongest and bravest boys could reach in the days when children still swam in the salt water here. The rock that cursed boats when the water was high. Like a sunken star. Sitting there like some beacon of light. A faulty light-house. Tonight — a surfacing eye, keeping watch over the Y as it fades into a fragmented dot-to-dot design. Lenny keeps watch. I slide the eight ball into park.

"Sure," Lenny says. "I'd let you ride my bike."

And I imagine filling the wire basket with rocks and sticks and things I find on the beach. Bits of broken glass and sea shells half filled with sea spit. Things have a way of washing up. Lenny told me that. I would keep an extra clothespin fastened to one side of the basket in case the one on my pant leg got lost. I would wave to Lenny as I rode away from his house where he sits on the front porch. I would laugh as I hear Lenny call out obscenities to me as I peddle away. I would ride Lenny's bike on the pavement because there are no sidewalks here. The gravel is much too rough to ride on, so I would ride on pavement where mothers push their baby carriages. No one seems to mind sharing the road with them. Besides, people don't mind slowing down for babies and retarded people.

I would ride all over town on Lenny's standard bike, braking only when I really needed to. Like when old people cross the

Wire Basket

road. I would peddle fast and hard to reach the cemetery that rests beyond the gravel pit. It has the best view of the town because it reveals the only opening in the valley walls. I would take my lunch from the wire basket on the front of Lenny's bike and sit down next to my grandfather. I would look at all the things Lenny and I pass when we drive in his truck. Things would look different if we were going slower and didn't have the music on so loud.

The religious hour comes on the radio and Lenny twists the tuner dial. Maybe the good reverend believes he will save the souls of the music lovers without them noticing. Bring Jesus into the sinners' lives right between the rock and the roll. We tune Jesus out and listen to the water tease the shore. Washing things up, carrying things out to sea.

We sit in Lenny's truck with the eight ball glued to the gear shift. We begin to name each star in the Y as we pull into gear and drive towards our falling sky.

Secrets

ANGELA HRABOWIAK

I WAS A DOG ONCE. That is my secret. I was also Isis, and could make the heavens spill their guts on the earth whenever I wanted them to. I could command deer and rabbits to surround me (this is before I understood the egotism inherent in the word "command"). I built a make-believe hut on the shores of our creek and pretended to live there through harsh winters, with one blanket and a flashlight, and no food other than what the Indians brought me. When the creek dried up, I could walk across it to the forbidden zone, and see my home from another perspective. I was Laura Ingles-Wilder's long-lost twin sister. I was magical and special. I'm still self-important and full of myself. Sometimes I love myself.

Secrets remind me of old ecru lace, tatted gracefully by gnarled, spotty hands with knuckles swollen through a lifetime's cold water and hard work. Secrets are akin to lies, and lies sink deeply into swamp-mud, covered for years until an enterprising barnswallow burrows through the silt to construct a half-shell nest of mud and secrets on brown barn beams.

A secret untold is like a drop of honey on the lips to a tongueless woman, sliding seductively out of reach down her chin. A secret untold remains a secret — told, it is lapped up greedily, swallowed.

My first year of secrets began the last day of school in grade seven. I was eleven then, and my favourite dress was made by

Secrets

Mumsy in bell-sleeved, empire-waisted material, swirls of lime green, tangerine, and coral, dancing the twist around my slim hips. I wore a dog collar as a necklace and fantasized daily about riding my horse to school, tying her up under the maple trees in the playground and bringing her sweet water during recess. I knew she'd toss her head and whinny thanks like Black Beauty, and wait patiently until the final bell rang when we could return home at a stately walk. I wondered whether it would be better to ride bareback, or leave her saddled the whole day. I opted for bareback. She'd be more comfortable, and the saddle would last infinitely longer — not exposed to rain, sun, and my trusty mare Bella's tendency to roll in the dust.

That summer I kissed the Renshaw twins, Cliff and Frank. Frank's lips were fuller than his brother's and his black, curly hair not so wild. Their eyes were blue. They were fraternal twins. I had a magical hold on them. I could make them do my bidding.

We spent fragrant afternoons lying on our backs, close-but-not-touching, admiring the blue skies, reluctantly going home at dusk with grass stains on our asses and ants in our shorts. They walked from their small clapboard house in York to our red-brick gingerbread farmhouse, sometimes kicking an old soup can the whole five miles of arid gravel roads. Occasionally, Mumsy drove me to their house, and we fished and swam the muddy green waters of the Grand River, plucking fat red leeches from our legs and never catching anything but snags of old wood, and water weeds, and feed bags filled with tiny corpses tied shut and tossed off-handedly into the water. We were chased by a farmer with a shotgun full of rock salt from his cornfield. We roasted marshmallows and ate them burned to charcoal crispness while mosquitoes and black flies sucked hungrily at our hot blood.

I could sleep all night, and snooze all day. A week had seven full days. Twice a week at least I'd climb the horse-chestnut tree in our front yard. Its arms were crooked and bent for maximum seating comfort. The leaves sheltered me from view. I could hide there for hours, until my skinny butt would go numb, and I'd have to stand for a while, flexing my muscles so I could navigate the branches on my descent. I'd knit or cork in my tree. I never actually made anything from the lengths of knit cord. It was enough to watch it grow and change colours as I'd add on new bits of scrounged yarn. Nothing matched, and it was all perfect.

That summer, I spent long hours with the farm animals — watching, touching, and smelling. The fresh air and the fruitful earth were my family. After all, I *was* Isis, and I could bark like a dog.

My dad said he'd shoot himself that summer. He drank a lot. I listened for gunshots from the barn. I learned to howl like a coyote.

The Summer Of Womanhood

ANGELA HRABOWIAK

THE SMELL OF summer's dying hung in the air, it bit at her nose like an ancient memory. Brilliant crimson sumach groves and a canopy of lemon-yellow maple leaves knocked at her dark brown eyes when her womanhood awoke. Although she didn't know it, she would look at the moment as a still-life masterpiece, framed in her mind in glossy gilt until the moment of her last heart beat.

There was nothing outstanding about the summer of her awakening. Most days passed with peanut-butter-and-jelly-sandwich steadiness. She slept as late as possible in the morning, comfy in her nakedness, covered only lightly by a flowered cotton sheet. She'd wake slowly, languidly, blurry in the late morning sun, while the dew evaporated from the long grass under the pear trees planted by gnarled workers' hands for the winter's sweet conserves. Wasps droned black-and-yellow marching songs as they made their way from pulpy windfall to sweet rotting fruit. Tea would be her breakfast of choice, milky and sweet (some mornings frothy bubbles foretold of fortunes to come — liars!).

The morning would unwind into afternoon while the sun rode a little higher in the blue Cayuga country sky. Cicadas would replace wasp drones, with their piercing multi-toned jazz trumpet blues. And she'd eat lunch. Sour cream, stacked high on rye bread, and a hot tomato just plucked from the garden would do just fine (or a grilled cheese sandwich, made with cheap white bread, toasted to cheese-melting crunchiness and dunked in plenty of ketchup).

She'd wander into the barn where she'd talk to the animals and smell the warm shit smell which overrode the sweetness of hay. The barn's darkness wrapped around her, cooling her sun-warmed skin, and the snuffling of the cows and horses would hypnotize her into resting from the labour of eating. She developed the ability to sleep standing, leaning against the corral, only occasionally finding herself melting to the ground.

After meditating in the barn, she'd wander back to the old farm house, and read her "Archie and Veronica" or "Fantastic Four" comics — bought for twelve cents at the variety store a country mile (and an hour's stroll) away. On good days, she'd find pop bottles in the ditch and she'd add a nickel to her day's spending money.

Onions, potatoes, tomatoes, and garlic would be waiting to be transformed from fresh garden produce to savoury supper, and the women of the house would begin the magical alchemy by first toasting the onions to nutty brown-ness. Supper would grow from their fingers as they orchestrated the foods on hand with the needs of the family. The calves they'd fed warm milk lay in the freezer, cut and wrapped, ready for eating, and those fluffy yellow chicks grew into roasting hens, ready to stuff for Sunday dinner.

Every other day or so, she and her mother would make a clean sweep through the house, picking up stray wisps of hay, straw, or chaff from the combining, and they'd nurse those nasty hay-bale scratches which just loved to plump up with juicy pus. Laundry would be gathered and separated into stinking piles of white, coloured, and grease-coated denim. The enamel white

The Summer of Womanhood

wringer washer would churn, and chug, and squeeze dirt and moisture from limp fabric. Laundry was washed in true conservationist style. White was first, as it was least dirty. Then, using the same water, the coloured laundry would be washed; and, in yet the same water, the denim would be washed (though, at this point, it was more like a redistribution of dirt in the soupy grey water). The sun would dry clothes hung on the line in the yard, near the pear trees. Ancient wood furniture would get yet another coat of lemon polish — God, she loved the sheen of old wood, freshly shining and fragrant, years glowing in the grain of table, once an oak, walnut or maple tree.

The days passed in humming sameness. Comforting and gentle like a lullaby goodnight. Her life would pass like other lives — birth, living, death. Seasons would change. Time would stroll past the home of her living (and may even rest there awhile). She'd be the same (only different) as the multitudes before her. Not much would change. She was a woman, like the women before her, and would be like the women after her. And she was a person, like every other person who ever was or would be.

But, underneath the reasoning and logic, her fibre, her being, her spirit knew the import of her existence, and valued the simplicity and divinity of being an ingredient in the soup of the world.

She was a woman. Now. There was no day to mark on the feed-store calendar. No event to pinpoint the transition. She would always remember this moment in perfect autumn, smelling the air like a doe. Underneath the perfection was an itchy twitch — a nagging awareness. A *thereness*. It was not as annoying as the labels those sadistic manufacturers sew on the back of clothing (forcing frantic monkey-arms akimbo back-scratching, turning like a dog chasing its tail). Nor did it needle away little jabs like an annoying burr in wool socks, but the *thereness* was present, strong and swollen.

She was a woman. Now. And forever, and dammit, she was here for the ride of her life. For the rest of her life.

Drag Marks

BETSY TRUMPENER

WHEN I WAKE UP, Farrell is nuzzling me, nibbling me. He says, "Mmm."

He licks my ear. He whispers, "I'll put the dogs out," like it's foreplay.

I say, "No, better not. They'll get into Klaus's truck. They'll get into the skulls."

I say, "I'll take them out. We'll stay out of the forest. We'll stick to the road. And if some wild thing attacks, I'll beat it off with their leash."

"Beat it with the leash?" asks Farrell, rolling over. "Lucky beast."

There are so many new positions you have to learn when you live out here. Cradling your neck and playing dead if it's a grizzly. Walking backwards, eyes downcast, whispering softly for a black bear. Acting brash and larger than life against a cougar. I sometimes practise these precautions in my head as if they were the steps in a fire drill, or the first-aid routine to stem fatal bleeding. But if it ever comes to that, I'm afraid I'll choose the wrong pose, or fumble with the bear spray, or forget how dead I'm supposed to play.

Drag Marks

In the winter, it's always dark here and I walk the dogs rather desperately, along the side of the barbed-wire forest, the lights of the house and the red-eyed pump shack retreating behind me. I walk down to the bottom of the forest, along an old abandoned road covered in frozen shit and our footprints buried under Klaus's truck tires. The dogs disappear under the wire and it's hard to see your footfalls in the dark. The only path is the colour of snow.

We disagree on the dangers out there, Farrell and I.

When Klaus came to stay the night, with his wife and his pumped-up truck packed down with green-tinged animal skulls still alive with maggots and the furs from his trapline on the Parsnip River, he was headed for the winter market back in Germany. But it seemed at first that he'd come here just to warn us.

Klaus told us to stay away from carcasses. He described the ragged circle of ravens we'd see in the sky, the cage of cow bones in the field beneath them, here a leathery leg still stuck to its hoof, there a half-smiling jaw bone.

The killer would be back to break the mouth of anyone hungry enough to feed, he told us.

It was night outside and we sat close together at our kitchen table. Our dogs, Samson and Lilly, lay on the brown scuffed linoleum and tea steamed in our hands and Klaus stroked his stocking feet across the top of the toes of Larissa, his quiet bride. I waited for Farrell to sigh or disagree, but he didn't. And I worried that perhaps we knew nothing about the harshness of this pastoral life, about the short, gasped screams of a rabbit carried away by a hawk. I felt I should get up and grab a pen and write warning notes on the skin of my hands. But when I made a move to get up, Klaus grabbed my arm. "Listen," he said. "This is vital." And I sat back down.

Klaus took a breath while we all held ours. "The only thing

more dangerous than a dead animal is a carcass that's there and then suddenly gone. Look for the drag marks," he said. "Watch your back. The killer is in hiding, waiting to pounce." Later, we all said good-night.

In the morning, Farrell got up and made breakfast for our guests before they headed to the airport with their fur. Klaus said he was hungry and I put out four spoons around the table but then Larissa said no, thanks or *Nein, danke,* or maybe she just shook her head. Farrell was cooking oatmeal on the stove with a wide metal spoon and he had his back to us. He didn't see how Klaus gave his wife a fierce look or how she twisted quickly away. He didn't see Klaus fake a punch at his wife's face.

Sometimes you don't see it coming.

It's spring now and the thaw is giving up its dead. The dogs sniff the raw air and bound ahead of us in the light. Farrell and I follow, hand in hand, down the bush road.

Farrell plans to pry up rocks for his collection with a little screwdriver. But on the way, we find the dead calf. A burst of red in the sunlight. Black-winged birds singing on a red rib, a patch of black fur, down in the ditch.

"Not pleasant," Farrell says, but anyway, he wants to look. He insists on it. He posts me like a nervous sentry, pleading, "Come on. Let's go. Let's go."

On the way home, we find a collared dog, still half-buried in snow. It's winter-stiff, a purple flower growing from its head.

I turn away and grab Lilly and kiss her flat on her liver mouth. I squat on the road with my nose in Lilly's fur. She smells like wet hay. I don't even think to look for drag marks.

To Dance in a Measured Space

SYBIL SHAW-HAMM

NOBLE DANCED with Marilyn Monroe — fifty-three years ago —
and never told until last Wednesday, just before lunch, and then
only after Madge raised the issue. Well, not the specific issue,
she couldn't raise that, could she? He hadn't told her yet.

For forty years, Madge and Noble Winston were farmers, but
aren't anymore. They retired — two years, six months and three
weeks ago. Shortly before they gave up farming Madge gave up
her job at the Kipner Herald. She'd worked there forty-six years,
writing local news. The Winstons have stayed put on their old
place; only the fields are rented out.

Now, most mornings right after breakfast, if Noble's bum leg
isn't acting up, he takes the half-ton to town. He goes for mail,
for milk, for the paper. "Going," he'll announce to Madge across
his last coffee. Then shoving his cup aside, he'll say, "You coming?" He always invites Madge along. In the beginning she went
but doesn't any more.

Last Wednesday morning, after the back door slammed shut,
Madge settled into her chair by the living-room window. As the
truck disappeared down the lane, the goings-on of Noble's morning took shape in her mind: *To the Co-op store. Pick up milk.*

"Why the milk first?" Madge used to argue this point with Noble.

To the Post Office. Stand around the lobby or on the front step if the weather's good enough, waiting for mail to be sorted, discussing CFL scores or how the local hockey is expected to do in the coming season. Or Morris, if he's there, may run through some curling shot he expects soon to be making.

"How's Morris?" Madge used to care how Morris was doing.

To the Pool Room. Play a game of snooker, find out which old boy is up to what.

"What are they up to?" Madge used to care what was going on.

To the Esso station. Fill in gas. Go inside for a paper. Tell whomever's around that he gets the paper for Madge — to keep her finger in the ink, haha. Esso Bert saying, Nobody does the local column like Madge Winston used to do it, no-sir-ee-no-bodee.

Madge has told Noble a dozen times not to bother with the paper anymore.

Then to Ed and Flossie's, stay fifteen minutes and start off for home.

The paper, the mail, the milk will be on the seat beside Noble. *If he hasn't left them sitting somewhere else.*

At 9:46, Madge levered herself from the chair by the living-room window and returned to the kitchen to wash up breakfast dishes. At 10:10, she tuned her radio to CBC Morning Side. She'd missed the news, but didn't care. At 10:20, she went to the bedroom and smoothed up bed covers. At 11:09, she arranged herself at the kitchen table. At 11:32, truck brakes squealed at the bottom of the lane. Noble had the phone bill with him, a litre of milk, and the paper. Halfway through the door, he began his morning report. "Saw Jessie at the Co-op. She's walking without her cane."

"Good."

"Ran into Doc Einarson; before flu season starts up we're to come for shots."

"Should."

"Bob, not in the poolroom. Guess he and Esther took off for Texas this morning."

"Nice."

"Dropped in at Ed and Flossie's." Madge knew he would.

After putting the milk in the fridge, Noble sat down at the table across from her and ripped open the phone bill. He glanced it over and set it aside. He then reached for the paper, worked it flat on the table and, sliding out the sport's section, shoved the rest in his wife's direction.

Madge had planned to ignore the paper that morning, but then caught glimpse of the Monroe story. Front page, bottom corner, in a two-column box, screened for easy seeing. Odd, them putting filler on a front page like that. Has to be filler, doesn't it? Marilyn Monroe can't be news; she's been dead too long.

"Well for Pete's sake, Noble, will you look at this, says here Burt Reynold's biographer claims Marilyn Monroe ..."

"I danced with her once."

Madge glanced at the calendar on the wall. Wednesday, tenth of September, 2002. She studied the clock beside the calendar. Eleven fifty-five. She gazed out the window and checked the day. A fine fall day. She stood up and moved towards the kitchen cupboards. She pulled open a door and picked out, from among six cans of chicken noodle soup, a can of tomato. She slid the can under the electric can opener and pressed the lever. Zip — the lid was off. Plop — a miniature silo of red soup hit the sauce pan.

"No noodle left?" Noble said, glancing up from his paper.

"None," Madge said and flung the empty soup can into the garbage bag. Muttering she grabbed the can back and splashed it full of water.

"No milk for the soup?"

"None."

"Thought I just brought some in."

The spoon whipped the heating soup. Noble got up and walked past Madge. He reached into the cupboard and took down two bowls and two spoons and the Noble & Madge mugs. Madge twisted around, snatched up the named mugs and shoved them back on the shelf. She yanked out two more — plain white. He set the table. They ate. Finished eating, she turned her cup handle to the east, her spoon handle to the west and studied the results. "Danced to what?"

"The Tennessee Waltz," said Noble.

Noble stood up. As he moved away, she gazed after him. By the back door he began to work his overalls over his going-to-town-clothes. While he wriggled he said something about fixing the damn squealing brakes. *But Noble, "The Tennessee Waltz," for Pete's sake! I was dancing with my darling to the Tennessee Waltz when an old friend I happened to ... For crying out loud Noble, our song, our dance, all these years, from our wedding dance in '48 'til Friday-last at the school, with Joe Langley resting down his fiddle and announcing it — Noble and Madge's Tennessee Waltz. Me laughing; you playing at being surprised. Us starting off, alone, together, across the sawdust on the oiled floor. My arm on your square shoulder. (So it slopes a little now.) My hand in your tough hand. (So it trembles a little now.) But still you. Still good old Noble. And me dancing along thinking I know all there is to know about you. You thinking what? Marilyn Monroe?*

These days on the Winston farm, when there's a crawling-under-the-truck job to do, Madge goes along with Noble to do it. She hands down tools, checks some of the cursing going on, sees he crawls out okay. But last Wednesday, after the dancing with

To Dance in a Measured Space

Marilyn Monroe news was given her, she wrapped herself in an old plaid jacket and stomped away from the garage towards the barn.

It was Noble who declared bush-walking — at their age — should be done on a beaten path. He was quick to add, "Not that anything's happened yet." The walking path begins just behind the barn, near a rose bush Madge set out years ago.

Last Wednesday, tugging the old plaid closer, she spoke to the bush in front of her. "Planted you five years ago — no — more like ten. And next summer, if you bloom again, I might be here to see; or I might not, and if not, who other than Noble will care?"

Finished having her say, she stomped on — along the path, into the poplars, to the oak tree where she stopped and looked up into its branches. *Gnarled old thing.* She swung a kick in the tree's direction. *Bull's eye.* A pain balled in her right hip, passed down her thigh into her knee. *Silly old fool.* "Damn," she cried aloud as she limped off. In time, she reached the edge of the bush, passed into the clearing and into the long grass meadow where the new spruce grove stood.

Some time ago, Madge had found Noble in the meadow, slicing ground open with his spade, slipping treelets in, stomping earth down on either side.

"More spruce trees, Noble?"

"Why not?"

"Years to grow."

"Five," Noble'd said.

"Wrong — twenty."

Noble had fallen then, face down on the ground. It had been all Madge could do to get him up and stagger him back to the house. Once on the couch, Noble declared, "Tomorrow always comes for somebody, Madge." But Madge knew he'd forgotten how slowly spruce trees grow. He'd forgotten.

That evening, as he rested, she went back to the grove and planted the remaining trees herself. Slice. Slip. Stomp. Finished planting, she'd piled the burlap sacks. Finished piling, she'd dragged the spade to the barn. On the way from the barn to the house, a pain clutched her gut. A pain that had nothing to do with the work she'd just done.

Now, standing in the new spruce grove, Madge said, "Well, there's no forgetting this time, is there, Noble? No siree, by a dozen drowning ducks, you couldn't blame your not telling on forgetting this time; not the way it popped from your mouth there at the table, easy as an egg out of a hen. Oh, you've always remembered this dancing business."

She turned then away from the small trees and retraced her steps through the meadow, across the clearing, into the poplar shade, past the oak tree, past the rose bush.

So you danced with Marilyn Monroe.

Madge didn't doubt Noble, and she didn't mind who he danced with; she'd never begrudged Noble his moments. *To "The Tennessee Waltz."*

She didn't care what he danced to, now she'd given it some thought, not really, not much.

And didn't tell until this morning.

Now this was the question arising in her: Did he tell before?

At the barn, an old church pew leans against the wall and Madge lowered herself down and considered who Noble might have told.

Him and Bob Penner in the marsh, sun rising in mist, morning air brisk, them hunkering down in bulrushes, scanning the sky for ducks, guns in hand, guns loosening their talk — man talk, war talk, Noble finally saying, One Christmas on Guam, I danced with Marilyn Monroe. Bob saying, Well, I'll be damned, who'd a guessed it, imagine us never hearing a good story like that before. Noble saying, Never told Madge, so it never got around.

Madge sighs.

To Dance in a Measured Space

Now Noble, would you say that about me?

"You bet he would."

If I'd known, would I have told?

"You bet I would."

Leaning back against the pew, Madge pictured how her own telling might have gone.

Us at a dance, and Flossie telling for the hundredth time how her Ed shot the hole-in-one and Esther bragging again how her Bob won The Stakes and me dropping it in — Noble danced with Marilyn Monroe. Flossie oohing. Esther ahhing. Both begging for the details.

"How can I give them details? Noble has them all."

So who gives a flying duck if he did tell Bob? Who gives a flying duck if he told the whole bleeding world? It's him telling me makes me so Billy-be-damned mad. Him telling me. Now.

Since retiring, Madge has tried to explain to Noble how she feels about Now. "Noble," she's said a dozen times, "for forty-six years I gathered up stories from this community and sorted them through and turned them into what people wanted to read in print, what they wanted to know about each other: wed to / born to / moved to / came home to / passed peacefully away from. But that was only part of it, only the skin. The rest, the real meat and bone stuff, I kept back, filed it away in me. Tons of it, Noble — their twistings and their turnings, their rages and their fears. In me, Noble. All that stuff they didn't want to know, didn't want written down. Too much of it, over too many years. So I figure, *Now*, is mine. All I ask is some space, some peace, maybe a few more sunrises, a few more summer roses, a few more walks to check the spruce trees. Simple things, Noble. No yesterday seeping back. No tomorrow fussing it up."

Noble argues back in his own way. "Going," he says every good morning. "Coming?" he asks every time. And, on the last

Friday of every month he reminds her about the Community Dance.

"Go yourself," Madge had snapped Friday-last. Then, as she stood at the sink washing up supper dishes, she saw Noble pacing out beside the barn and, for the first time, she took in the slope of his shoulders. A half-hour later, Noble found Madge sitting at the table, her dancing skirt on.

On the way to the dance, Madge again tried to explain herself. "No more people, no more stories, no more surprises; no more changes — if we can help it. Enough already. Nothing more."

Out in the pew, resting in the late afternoon sun, Madge asked herself why Noble has chosen now to tell her his Marilyn Monroe business.

Why now does he drop me this tidbit?

She considered for a minute.

To lure me back to story land is why. To get me back pounding the old Remington is why. To give me a recharge, to have one thing lead to another, as if he thinks he knows me that well.

Madge knows Noble brags that she can change her mind faster than greased lightning. She knows he tells how she can turn around any place, any time, on the head of any dime if she decides to.

She felt a sudden need for Noble, a need to see his shape, a need to hear his voice. She knew exactly where he would be.

In the kitchen. Coffee ready. A bag of Oreos sitting out. The Noble & Madge mugs side-by-side on the table. And when the back door slams he'll call out that the truck is fixed if I need it. And when I come into the kitchen he'll ask if I want coffee.

"So, why, Madge Winston, are you out here digging in your heels? Why are you sitting here scuffing your toes?" Turning,

Madge gripped the arm of the bench. Up; and she moved across the yard. Inside; and she let the back door slam.

"Truck's fixed if you need it."

She slipped off the old plaid, tossed it towards the wall hook and ambled into the kitchen.

"Coffee?"

She sat down at the table, sighed, coughed, and picked up the Madge-mug.

Never appear too eager.

Sighed, smiled, and held out the mug for Noble to fill.

Somewhere nearby a deadline pressed in on her. But she knew better than to say.

When you're after details, never, never let the deadline show.

In An Ordinary House

KIM SCARAVELLI

THE FIRST SIXTEEN years of my life were spent in a vinyl-sided Cape Cod at 6758 Hope Crescent. The house numbers were stencilled in burgundy on an oval plaque to the right of the front door — also burgundy. Tiny, tole-painted flowers encircled the numbers and the blue of the blooms matched the shade of the siding. Flat-topped shrubbery lined the front walkway and a short, white picket fence ensured that visitors never strayed off the path to endanger the well-tended Kentucky bluegrass. Everything about the house on Hope Crescent co-ordinated. Mother was dedicated to the development of colour themes and the strategic placement of accent pieces. Each room was designed with purpose — the living room "toned down" with a limited number of earth tones and the kitchen "cheered up" by a broad spectrum of "related" yellows. Bananas had to be kept in the breadbox because Mother insisted that they clashed.

Maybe that was my problem. I clashed. Mother and Father were both tall and willowy with Nordic features — striking was the term that came to mind when they strode into rooms together. Bright blue eyes, chiselled features, long straight noses and long, thin necks. My sister, Francine, was a cookie-cutter copy of Mother. I seemed to have come from an entirely different batch of dough.

At sixteen, I stood barely five feet in my shoes and I blended well with the living room — brown hair, brown eyes, brown freckles scattered across a broad expanse of beige skin. My face was round and flat, the bridge of my nose so slight that my glasses had no place to perch and I was continually sliding them up with the tip of my index finger. My head sat firmly on my shoulders, with such little space between chin and chest that Mother would buy only mock turtlenecks for fear of emphasizing the situation. I was expressly forbidden to tuck in these mocks because, as Mother told me a million times, "The last thing you want to do is draw attention to the waist." There was really very little to draw attention to — my middle was flat and straight — no curving out at the top, no curving in at the middle and only the slightest curve out at the bottom.

"Potato-shaped," Mother would whisper to sales girls as she enlisted their assistance. It was one of her tireless missions to search out "something decent" for me to wear. My body was an obstacle to be overcome — a public embarrassment.

I had no objection to burying myself inside while Mother, Father and Francine strode tall through the social world. To stand beside them in church or at a town function was the ultimate display of my failure. A nervous sweat would make my hands cold and clammy and my heart would pound so heavily within my head that I wouldn't be able to hear the words of those around me. I would fall outside of the conversation, aroused only by the sharp jab of Mother's bony elbow against the soft fleshi- ness of my rib cage. "Speak up, Feona," she would purr, sliding a smile towards whatever neighbour may have spoken to me. But I would have no idea what to say and would be left with only a lame grin and a mumble or two to add to the dialogue.

"She's just shy, our Feona. Don't know what we're going to do with her." A soft, well-manicured hand would come to rest lovingly upon my shoulder, a mother nurturing her poor, feeble-minded child. Slowly, the grip would tighten, until a searing heat spread across my shoulder blades and I stood silently and painfully admonished.

I can see so clearly now the way I feared my mother, the way I shrank under her disapproving gaze, the way my body stiffened at her touch. Yet, when she grew ill, it was me, only fourteen at the time, who struggled hardest to keep her in the world of flesh and bones. Father couldn't seem to bear the sight of her, although I wrapped silky turbans around her balding head and brushed powder on her cheeks right up to the end. He would scurry off to work as early as possible and retreat into the study before I had cleared the dinner plates off the table. At eight o'clock each evening, he would come to stand outside the bedroom door, one hand on the doorknob and the other steadying him against the frame. I would peek down the stairwell and watch him gathering himself, pushing down the fear, curling up the corners of his lips, pasting a smile firmly on his face before turning the knob.

"Good evening, sweetheart," he would boom. "I've been thinking of you all day." His voice grew louder each week as he hollered to be heard above the cancer, above the pills, above the hopelessness. And then the door would close and I would sit in silence at the top of the stairwell, waiting for him to reach his fill. The nightly visits became shorter and shorter until, in the final days, I imagined that I could see his hand still gripping the knob on the inside of the door, not entirely letting go of the so-much-better world outside.

When he left, I would return to deal with Mother. Bodies are like old cars, I guess. The closer to the junk heap, the heavier the maintenance. Cleaning, clothing, medicating — the days were eaten up as surely as her body and in the last few weeks I abandoned all attempts at school and even took to sleeping on the floor beside her bed — so as to be there when the time came.

Francine was good to me then. She knew that I was carrying the burden for us both and while she couldn't bring herself to share the load, she tried to compensate by pampering me a bit. Tiny, foil-wrapped chocolates would appear on my pillow. My favourite orange bubble bath would turn up in the wicker basket beside the bathtub. Trashy magazines would find their way into the grocery bags. She even made dinner a few times, although her culinary skills were sadly lacking. I started preparing meals in larger amounts and freezing them, since her thawing was less dangerous than her cooking.

On the day that Mother left us, I baked a ham. It made a simple dinner for that first evening, when we sat in numbed silence in our cheerful yellow kitchen. It serviced the following days well, as a seemingly endless parade of mourners passed through that burgundy door. Yes, I would recommend ham to anyone in a time of distress — it's solid, hearty meat and it stretches as far as the need.

I grew quite adept at baking ham. Pork tenderloin, pot roast, liver smothered in onions ... I had all the red meats mastered in the year following Mother's departure. I also had the kitchen repainted — a crisp, clean white with a multi-coloured border that I picked up on a whim. Covered in a mass of unnamed flowers, it wrapped itself around the room and welcomed all the shades of the rainbow into my little retreat. I slowly collected a drawer full of tablecloths and placemats in all sorts of patterns and changed them weekly, although I was the only one who took any notice.

Life fell into a comfortable, steady rhythm in that first year. School, cooking, cleanup, homework — dusting on Saturdays and laundry on Sundays while Father and Francine were out. Without Mother's iron will, all attempts to drag me out of the house quickly dissolved and I was left to myself most of the time. Father took more and more of his meals in front of the television and Francine seemed to give up eating altogether. Things were good. I was even considering wallpaper for the living room.

Then one wet and windy Sunday morning — a real nasty one, with rain pounding the kitchen windows and a fierce wind hollering down the stove vent — well, on that one inclement Sunday, I happened to catch Francine tying up the belt of her all-weather coat. It was like I hadn't really stopped to look at her — really look at her — in a long, long time, and I was shook through to my bones by how much she had changed. That coat tie left ends so long that she had to knot them into a fancy bow just to keep them from hanging longer than the hem of the coat. And the fingers that buttoned her buttons were shaky, with knobby white knuckles standing out like the knots on a tree branch.

Father didn't seem concerned. He put his arm around her bony shoulders and threw the both of them out into the driving rain. I heard his voice booming "Just a second, sweetheart," as he fumbled to unlock the car door. Then they were gone. As they faded down the driveway, I could see Father's mouth moving. Perhaps he was singing along with the radio. But Francine sat still as a photograph, her face blank and her sallow cheeks splattered with raindrops.

I got a funny feeling, deep down in my centre, a bad feeling that made me want to grab my umbrella and make a dash for the car. But I had a shepherd's pie all ready to go into the oven and biscuit dough rolled out on the counter. So I ran my sweaty palms under warm tap water and went back to my affairs.

I tried not to think about Francine. I experimented with new recipes and sewed a valance for the kitchen windows. I even started cleaning out the hall closet, where I planned to put in some shelving and start a jam pantry. But suddenly, I found myself painfully aware of her presence. Her body gave off an odour of misery that clung to the furniture and lingered in the air long after she had moved on. She stopped going out, except with Father. The weight loss became increasingly worrisome and she grew out her bangs until they covered her eyes like heavy draperies. I tried to start conversation, hoping to draw her out of her ever-thickening shell. But our words had always been widely spaced and heavy.

"How's the pork?" I would ask, beaming my brightest smile across the table.

"Great." Francine would mumble back, busily spearing small bits of meat and burying them under her mashed potatoes.

"I let it soak in beef consommé for a while. Really makes a difference." I would charge headlong into the details of the meal until both myself and the topic were completely exhausted. Then we would slide back into the familiar silence of our dinner table. As soon as possible, she would push back her chair and slip away to her bedroom.

Father, who generally ate at a TV table in the living room, would glance over his shoulder as she passed by. "Where are you off to in such a rush?" he would ask in an oddly plaintive voice, the question resolved by the solid thud of the bedroom door. So Father would sit alone in the dark, outlined by the blue glow of the television. And I would clean the kitchen, spread my homework out across the tablecloth and make myself a cup of tea.

Each night repeated the same ritual, with Father still glued to the screen when I finally headed off to bed. I would sometimes hear him puttering about, making messy midnight forays into my kitchen. He would leave buttery knives on the counter and forget to put the cheese back in the refrigerator. "Absent-minded," I told myself, banishing less generous adjectives.

Father had always lived in the shadows of our house. Without Mother, he was lost and disoriented, shuffling about from room to room. Only Francine seemed to bring the light back into his eyes. He became terribly interested in her comings and goings, wanting to drive her everywhere, willing to wait outside the mall or the library for as long as her errands took. Oddly, although he devoured her with attention, he didn't seem to notice her weight loss or the flat whiteness of her cheeks. Father chased, Francine ran. Her trips out of the house became limited to school and church and he had to resort to bribery and threats just to lure her into the living room on an evening.

"Come on in and watch with me, Frannie. You pick the program. You can have the whole sofa to yourself if you want." On the rare occasion, she would surrender to his pleas, positioning herself in the tiny corner chair, a seat so small that Mother had always considered it more accent-piece than furniture. Francine would fold herself in half, finding space on the tiny cushion for her feet as well as her frighteningly narrow backside. She would turn off the standing lamp and wrap her arms around her shins, keeping her face low against her knees. I imagine that's what those girls who jump out of cakes must look like just before the bachelor party yells "Surprise." There were certainly no surprises waiting at the end of an evening with gloomy Francine — just a long stretch of sullen silence before she vanished into her room.

Despite my outpouring of well-balanced meals, I never seemed to catch Father's attention. It wasn't that he was mean or inconsiderate. No, he was always polite and well mannered. He shared his gentlemanly postures with me just as he did with neighbours who passed him on the street. In time, I came to see how hopeless the situation was. I would never have the quality that most drew him to Francine. She was the mirror image of Mother and no amount of self-deprivation or denial could cover those always-striking features. I accepted what I could not change and took comfort in my world of recipe cards and closet renovations.

It was my quest for information on sauces and condiments that found me in the secluded space at the top of the stairwell one rainy evening. I was determined to recreate Mother's famous Cornish game hen. Armed with only a flashlight, I had squeezed into the crawl space on the second-floor landing, where the attic stairs met the hallway. This is where all the cookbooks, photo albums, and other uglies were kept. Mother couldn't stand the clutter of such things, but her practical nature made her a natural collector of reference guides.

Father was downstairs watching television and Francine was burrowed in her room. The house was silent and peaceful and I became so engrossed in my culinary explorations that the distant creak of the kitchen cupboards shocked me a bit and sent tiny shivers up my spine. In a second, I realized that it was only Father meandering about in search of a late night snack. I crawled nearer to the stairwell and was about to go downstairs and help him when he emerged triumphant, a small wooden tray held out in front of him. As he moved to the part of the hall best illuminated by the glow of the television, I was surprised to see a tiny vase on one corner of the tray, accented with two red carnations blatantly stolen from the centrepiece on my kitchen table.

Instinctively, I slid back into the shadows and watched as Father moved past the living room, with its well-worn recliner and soothing earth tones. He walked gingerly, focusing on the contents of the tray and careful not to tip the vase. Then, slowly, his destination reached, he lowered the tray to the floor outside of Francine's bedroom door. He stood, one hand on the doorknob and the other steadying his form against the frame. With a certain sense of déjà vu, I watched him gathering himself and waited for that moment when the knob would turn. But Father's hand did not turn the knob of this door. Instead, he pressed his face close against the wood and whispered hoarsely.

"Let me in, Francine." Moments passed. His hand turned the knob. The movement was so slight that it created only an insignificant clicking noise. "I've got some cheese and crackers. Let me in, Francine." With another involuntary spasm, the hand jerked and the knob clicked, but Father remained alone in the hallway. "I'm going to come in," he whispered, seeming to inform himself of his plans. I focused all of my attention on that hand, but the knob was still.

Then the door creaked open a sliver, the final turn coming not from his rough and trembling hand, but from a softer, smaller version within the room. There was furtive whispering and the door slowly acquiesced, allowing Father to step inside. Then he was gone.

I sat there in the darkness for a while. Waiting. Eventually, I rose and walked the miles between my darkened stairwell and that sinister door frame. I remember placing my own hand on the knob and feeling its cold strength. I could not turn that knob.

And so, I gathered up the untouched tray and went down the stairs and into my kitchen. I returned the red carnations to their rightful place in the bouquet and tidied up Father's mess. Then I sat at the table and listened to the comforting sounds of the room itself — the steady hum of the refrigerator, the tinkling of the baseboard heaters. I imagined that I could even hear the padding of tiny feet as a mouse beneath the floorboards made his way to the cheese chunks in the garbage bin under the sink. I pictured him in a little nightgown and hat, dancing along on his back legs with a miniature candleholder and a speck of flame lighting his way. I enjoyed my childlike fancy for a moment, but there was not enough of the child left within me to hold the picture clear. Soon I came to hear only the sickening sound of a rodent scurrying about. I made a mental note to buy traps and poison in the morning and I found my way to bed.

The night was very long and the silence of the morning even longer. The awkwardness could only be avoided by remaining solitary and so we swiftly and silently divided the house, sharing only stairs and hallways. In keeping with our new boundaries, I found myself humming alone in the kitchen on a bright Saturday morning, with Francine upstairs digging through the crawl space for the answer to some unknown question and Father in his now-traditional spot in front of the television.

In an Ordinary House

I was making pancakes, enjoying the steady beating of the batter. There were apples simmering on the stove. I wiped my hands off on a yellow gingham towel before grabbing the cinnamon off the spice rack. I sprinkled the apples until the sauce turned honey brown in the pot and a heady scent rose from the stove. As an afterthought, I tossed a liberal dose into the batter as well and then went back to my beating. Cinnamon is not one of my favoured spices — strong and overpowering — it smothers the natural taste of the food. But Father always liked it and I truly wanted him to savour his pancakes.

I lay a linen napkin across the tray — deep blue and scattered with a pattern of tiny red blossoms. I put the pancakes on a red plate, to accentuate the colour of the flowers, and generously spooned the warm applesauce over the top. It was a beautiful display. Father's eyes never left the screen, but his hands found their way to the knife and fork and he dug into his pancakes right away. I wasn't feeling much like eating and so I left him there and went back into my kitchen.

There was batter splattered everywhere, already hardening on the counter and in spots along the backsplash. I snapped on my yellow vinyl gloves and scrubbed until I felt a trickle of perspiration between my breasts. Finally, I worked to free my sweaty hands and tossed both the gloves and the gingham tea towel into the garbage. I looked around and took long, deep breaths of the freshly cleaned kitchen. Then I poured myself a tall glass of juice and assumed my position at the kitchen table to rest ... and to wait.

I waited for a long time. The juice grew warm and the smells of cinnamon and disinfectant mingled together and faded away. Finally, I heard Francine's catlike movements on the stairs and her frantic mewing sounds in the hallway.

"Feona! Feona! Get in here." I rinsed my glass out in the kitchen sink and smoothed the front of my dress. Then I followed the sound of her voice, now a whisper rather than a scream. She was still standing in the hall, not moving any closer to Father. He was face down on the floor in front of the recliner, his body covering the now-collapsed TV tray. I could see no sign of left-over pancakes. We stood together for a moment, sharing the view. Then she sprang to life and rushed past me to the telephone.

The rest of the day was very busy. Father and Francine went out together, he all white and silent on the gurney, she suddenly finding her powers of conversation, babbling madly to every uniform. There were neighbours lining the walkway, jumping over the fence and crowding onto the grass. I felt Mother's disapproval of the situation but couldn't imagine a way to get rid of the noise or the confusion. Finally, amid the chaos, an older officer stepped towards me, offering to exchange my slippers for a practical pair of worn, brown loafers retrieved from the mat by the front door. It was a gentlemanly gesture and I smiled in appreciation. I allowed him to help me into my coat and I remember the warmth of the protective arm he slipped around my shoulders as he led me through the crowd and into his waiting car.

I live in a new place now — beautiful gardens and a wonderful solarium where I can sit for hours and collect my thoughts. I am discouraged from wandering into the huge, colourless kitchen on the ground floor, but the cook is friendly and we have exchanged a few recipes. Folks here seem intent on hearing every detail about those sixteen years on Hope Crescent. It's disconcerting sometimes — so much attention focused on my words. I tell them about Mother, about the house and the colour schemes. But there are some things that I know belong behind closed doors. "Family matters," Mother used to say. "Nobody's business but our own."

The Medicine Cabinet

KATHY MAGHER

NAN LAUGHED AT ME the day I took my first plunge into the bowl.
When she saw how startled I was, she told me it happened to
her all the time, that I should be careful to check that the seat
was down because of Dad, and then she asked me if I wanted to
hear a secret. I sat on the toilet, my feet dangling, and I listened
as Nan opened the medicine-cabinet door and showed me what
was there.

Nan and I often shared the bathroom. There was just enough
room for one person sitting and one person standing in front of a
sink that was too low for an adult. Tiny bathroom, but it seemed
roomy to me then. The wooden medicine cabinet hung just above
the sink. A tall, narrow window let the light in from the west and
the view looked across the sloping tin roof of our house, across
the honeysuckle and lilac trees, to the village church steeple in
the distance. A small, claw-foot bathtub filled the rest of the
space. Saturday-evening bath time meant that I lay stretched
head to toe in that four-foot tub, feeling lucky that I was soaking
in the last of the hot water from the now-empty tank. The setting
sun often accompanied me during those luxurious summer-
evening baths and the church bells sounded like a symphony.
That's when I was most happy about living in the village. Life in

Fremonton stretched out across the valley and the farmland lay beyond, along the rolling hills.

"Don't empty the water. I'm next," Dad shouted.

My time had just about run out. If I stayed much longer the water would be cold. Unfair to Dad. Worse, he could come in and begin shaving and that would mean that he would need to open the medicine cabinet to retrieve his razor and shaving brush. Then I would have to be careful to keep my eyes away, fearing I would be pulled into the story that had settled on the inside of the medicine-cabinet door.

The inside of the medicine-cabinet door had a poster stuck to it. The words *Auction. Farm for Sale* were printed across it. There was a boy, sitting cross-legged, tears pouring down his face. In his sorrow he was bidding farewell to his most beloved, his horse. He caressed the horse's face which was bowed low for affection. Beautiful and helpless. I said to Nan that it was only a picture, but she assured me it was more than that. She said there was a true story behind it. I asked her how she knew and she said she just knew.

"Is it Black Beauty?" I would ask Nan.

Sometimes, but not always, she would answer "yes." Otherwise the story remained the same.

"This is the boy's horse."

"Why is he crying?" I asked.

"They have to sell the farm."

Nan went on to tell me that the woman standing in the distance was the boy's mother. She was standing inside the half-door of a stable, looking out at her son, with her fleshy arms resting on the doors. She was round and motherly, plainly dressed, sullen, staring blankly at the boy's heartbreak.

"They're going to sell his horse," Nan continued.

Then it would happen. I'd start to cry, transported into the medicine-cabinet world, convinced. It smelled of Vicks and Noxzema, cough syrup and oils and shaving lotions, hair ointments, iodine, muscle creams, and arthritic healing potions. It was filled with small brown bottles of untouchables bearing my father's name and some with my mother's name. Dad kept them there even after she died. But mostly, that medicine cabinet was filled with the boy's heartache. When I had cried long enough for Nan's satisfaction, she would relieve me by closing the door and fastening it with the tiny hook, safely stowing the medicinal odours along with the horror that went on there.

On those rare occasions when I would witness Dad shaving, I would never stay very long and often succeeded in leaving before he let the story escape. Not that Dad discussed the medicine-cabinet story. He didn't have to. I was quite sure of his stance. I silently wondered why he allowed this injustice to occur. I blamed him in his adulthood, an onlooker just like the boy's mother. Surely something could be done.

"Why don't they just keep the horse for the boy?" I asked Nan in desperation.

"They can't afford it. They have to sell the horse," Nan explained.

And each time I dared look inside, sometimes afraid that the scene might have progressed, I always found time floating precariously on this same point of inevitability. Yet I continued to imagine it to be changeable somehow.

I have been to many auctions growing up here. It's the thing to do on a summer Sunday. The whole parish attends, usually right after Sunday mass. The year I turned thirty-three, Dad had an auction. When he invited Nan and me to come and claim whatever treasures we might like, I wasn't sure then what was most precious to me. There were worthless, priceless things, like my mother's tin bucket of buttons that I was so fond of as a little girl. I put this aside to keep. There were beautiful things, like her old Singer sewing machine — the kind you had to pump with your two feet — that years later I would come to miss more than I thought I would that day of the auction. It seemed that the things that had once formed part of my life, now laid out before me for sale, had taken on an obtuse quality once removed from the spaces they had always filled. Then I remembered the medicine cabinet. It was still there, in the bathroom. I was happy it wasn't part of the selling. I sat on the toilet, able to reach it without much of a stretch. Tiny bathroom. I was anxious to see the boy again — anxious and apprehensive. When I opened the cabinet door, the church bells sounded, and the boy was gone. The interior of the medicine cabinet had been painted. The scene was buried beneath a single coat of white satin. Even the smells were gone.

Then I heard a knock. It was Nan. "Hurry!" she said. "The auctioneer is here!"

All that remained was the faint outline of the boy's face, seemingly ghostlike now, staring at me as I sat on the toilet. Crying.

Mermaids

K. Linda Kivi

AT FIRST, Margaret didn't register the sound. It came as an inaudible tune, a reedy voice carried in by the evening breeze off the cove, more a presence than anything else. It seeped through weathered clapboard and grizzled stone alike, permeating Margaret's dreams. It caused her — and undoubtedly others in Stirling — to smile without knowing why. On the icy streets, the village folk looked up into the budless winter trees and claimed that spring was in the air though it was only February. People looked over their shoulders, scribbled circles in the gravel road with their stiff shoes, pulled their coats tightly around themselves, then undid them again.

At first, Margaret paced. Later, the sound lured her out along the road that skirted the cove and ended at the lighthouse point. But still, she didn't know why.

This day was no different. Like the other times she marched to the point, her brisk step kept time to unknown forces as her petticoats and skirts flicked in the wind. It was as though she was caught in a large drift net that was being drawn in.

The worst was that she had to pass Georgina McPhillip's house, there where the cove narrowed and fishing boats squeezed through. Each time she approached the clapboard house — the last in a row of dilapidated, greying houses —

Margaret set her eyes on the lighthouse beyond to keep herself from catching sight of it out of the corner of her eye.

Georgina's house was set back from the road and even those who didn't know who lived there said the house had a haphazard, mocking air to it, as if the ridge pole were a satisfied smile. The rain-bleached wood trimmings on the porch blazed like bared teeth. It had not been this way when Georgina's uncle was still alive.

No. It was *that woman*, Margaret thought as she strode past without looking back, who had made it so. Who knew what state the interior was in. Georgina, with her continental ways, never invited people from the village in. Margaret gritted her teeth. How could anyone be so proud of their impropriety as to flaunt it as she did: those terrible cheroots she smoked, laughing high and loud at men's stories; it was even rumoured that she drank wine with her meals.

And there was simply no looping her into place. Georgina had returned to Stirling after her operatic career expired ten years earlier. She had become an aggravating splinter under Margaret's nail, too embedded to remove and too niggling to ignore. And Margaret knew that Georgina went out of her way to provoke her. The looks. The refusal to take interest in the things other women did.

All except the singing. And the church choir wasn't good enough either. No. Georgina had to be a diva. Draw everybody's attention with her flashing laugh and tight bodice. And then, finally, she had escaped to the Continent where she sang on stage from Pompei to Manchester, they said. But what kinds of public places were they? Shoddy dance halls where men spit tobacco into the aisles? Margaret did not know enough to imagine venues of velvet curtains and the muffled clapping of gloved hands.

The nerve of Georgina to come back. The nerve.

Walking past Georgina's house made Margaret forget her

restlessness, if only for a moment. *I have lived a good and virtuous life,* she reminded herself, placing one black buttoned boot in front of the other.

I have lived — Yes, just put her out — a good and virtuous life — of my mind, she repeated to the rhythm of her steps.

But the sound, it was harder to dispel. Because Margaret could not put her finger on it, could not say, this is the sound of the sea, or, this is the sound of Mr. McQuarry's fiddle, or ...

Maybe it was the mermaids ...

Pshaw! It was unspeakable. Her blasted dreams had put the thought in her mind. The memory of those half-clad, slippery women filled Margaret's thoughts and quickened her pace. The other night there had been four women — four sirens — washing each other's hair in the sea foam. Always laughing while they sang. Always coaxing her, coaxing her down the rocks to the water's edge.

No. NO! She wouldn't think of them; she tightened her lips and leaned into the ocean's gusty wind. She forgot her feet. She forgot the lighthouse. She tried to put Georgina out of her mind.

But the thoughts refused to leave. They demanded her attention and took it. Just took it.

Margaret rounded the last curve before the open sea. Perhaps the sun would bake her clean. It was full and hot on her face and she didn't care, for once, whether her nose would freckle. The incessant rain of Stirling's winter seemed to harbour dangerous thoughts. She needed a day like this, a high blue sky and a fierce wind to tear at her skirts and wipe her mind clean.

She passed the lighthouse and picked her way over the rocks above the high tide line. The sea was whipping in a fury, the white lace of wind on the tips of the waves. If the men had any sense, they'd be fishing closer to the shore today. She scanned the horizon for their boats but it was as speckless as the sky. And, of course, there were no mermaids to be seen.

Margaret had never been out on the open sea. Her boating

had been restricted to the cove where, when she was younger, she would allow her suitors to row her about and make polite conversation. This was good. She was not one to go into the woods or over the hill past the cemetery. The cove was in full sight. No man would be taking advantage of her. Never. Even after she married Cedric Hawkins, she made it clear that the bed was a place for slumber and bearing children. That and nothing more. Nothing more.

Georgina, on the other hand, behaved like the wild sea wind. At first, Margaret had excused her, orphaned as she was at twelve and raised by her bachelor uncle. A girl needs a mother, a guiding light. But, even after Georgina's uncle had sent her to the convent school in Sydney, stories of Georgina's pranks continued to filter back to Stirling. Mrs. McQuaid's niece, who boarded at the school one winter, said that Georgina had forced a second-form girl to dance on a dining-room table while she played the spoons. Georgina had been punished, of course.

Even so, the Sisters had been too good to her. They had gathered funds for Georgina to study music abroad. Imagine. And though they had sent dull Emily along to keep Georgina in line, the stories that Em returned with proved that Georgina was trouble.

It was in Europe that Georgina had begun to smoke those terrible brown cigarettes and to galavant about with who knows who. It was no wonder that she lost her voice. A saucy girl like her didn't deserve to sing like an angel, high and trilling, so clear and bell-like that even Margaret had to admit it was beautiful.

Beautiful, Margaret thought, gazing out across the water, especially when Georgina sang about the sea.

The sea. The wild grey churning scoured Margaret's thoughts like ashy suds in the bottom of a burnt pot. Margaret could have stood there for hours but the men would be home soon. They must not see her. She would not be talked about like Georgina was, skulking about the cliffs, waving the flaps of that outrageous cape of hers in the salty gusts. Sometimes the men floated home into the cove with smiles on their faces, each and every one holding dear some secret they thought their wives would never divine.

Margaret would have suspected nothing had her youngest not blurted the men's secret. It was his first time at sea with his father and could not help but bubble with excitement, "I heard her, Mother. I heard ..."

Margaret's husband shushed the boy before he could say more. Did he think she was stupid? She stole down to the lighthouse every afternoon for a week before she saw her: Georgina's tall figure perched on the precipice next to the lighthouse, her dark, shiny hair loose and flapping like silken undergarments on a clothesline. As the boats came in, she sang to them. The song was a lament, an Irish tune about a woman whose love was lost at sea. From behind the low clump of heather where Margaret crouched, she could hear slips of the mournful song that were carried her way by the wind. Finally, she escaped, flushed and stern after the dreadful spectacle was over.

Now she studied the rocks and hills above her. It would not do to run into Georgina now. But, Margaret consoled herself, *that woman* was probably still in bed, smoking cheroots and drinking her tea without milk. Sloth was the devil's playground. Still, one could never be sure. It was important to be sure.

She peered over the edge of rocks to ensure that the coast was clear.

One day in spring, Margaret was out on one of her walks to the point. The men had returned early, drifting into the cove through the opaque fog, worried they would smash their boats against unseen rocks or worse yet, lose their direction out in the open waters. After they unloaded and cleaned their flapping cargos of glassy-eyed fish, they set to work repairing torn nets. There was time enough to walk to the point and back before Cedric and the children would be ready for their supper.

Margaret's pace was slower this day, the fog so thick she couldn't see beyond the foot that was leading. With the warm fog, a certain wetness permeated. Margaret walked in the tall grasses between the tracks, preferring to gather the dampness of their stems into her skirt than risk the slick mud of the ruts. She was so concentrated on the task of putting one foot safely in front of the other that she would not have noticed she was near Georgina's had it not been for a sound.

The sound ...

Through the fog came a low, deep thrumming, not one-two-three, but rhythmically, musically, as if to accompany other instruments. As she drew parallel to Georgina's house, the higher notes of the music took their places.

Margaret stopped, stunned. There were three or four instruments, and singing too. Georgina could not do this all on her own. Where had the musicians come from? No one had told her of visitors to Stirling. No unknown carriages had passed her house on the only street of the village. No strangers had been seen; Margaret would have been informed.

She strained to hear the voice, to pick out the instruments. She stepped off the dewy rise between the ruts and took a few steps towards the house. There was a piano, something like a fiddle, but different. And the low sound. It was a tune that she did not recognize, a sweet melody and a woman's high voice that did not sound like Georgina's. Margaret knew Georgina's voice so well. Too well.

How had this happened?

Margaret's lips shrunk away from the smile that had threatened to emerge. *That woman.* How had her guests eluded Margaret? It would not do. Not do.

Margaret turned and marched back home in as dignified a manner as possible, given the fog, given the circumstances.

Mermaids

That night Margaret dreamt of mermaids again, their glossy hair cascading down around their indecent breasts. Seven iridescent fish tails flicking unspeakable invitations. She woke up with a burning in her belly and dispelled it with resolve. She would find out just who these people were who had snuck into Stirling without so much as a nod to the decent people who lived there.

"Outrageous!" Mrs. McQuaid was sufficiently shocked by the news when Margaret ushered her first guest into the sitting room. The good women of Stirling came one by one, as was their custom, to their weekly tea-and-sewing party. The others were equally surprised.

"No. I knew nothing of this," Mrs. Smythe insisted. "Though there has been something strange in the air these past few months. Don't you agree?" The sitting women nodded.

"I'm not surprised it has to do with Georgina," another added. "She does have the habit, so to speak, of the unconventional."

"But that house of hers is so tiny," Margaret interjected. "Where could they all possibly ..." Margaret covered her mouth and glanced around the room as if to measure how shocked the others would be, "... well ... where do they sleep?"

The room succumbed to a deep silence.

"Perhaps they are all women," tiny, quiet Mrs. McDaniel offered.

"I heard a low instrument. And at least two fiddles, or something like it."

"Violins," Mrs. Smythe, who had studied in Halifax, offered. "And the low sound — probably a bass, but a woman does not play a bass."

Margaret raised her eyebrows, looked at the others as if to

say "see." They nodded in assent.

"I wonder if they all smoke cheroots?" Mrs. McDaniel asked, in a wistful tone.

The others silenced her with stern glances.

Oh, it wouldn't be so bad, Margaret thought, as they all pricked the taut cloth of their embroidery hoops, if Georgina was their own private disgrace. But no. People who otherwise would never have heard of Stirling, knew of it only because of Georgina. How many Nova Scotian divas had graced the stages of Europe? Only one. Regrettably, only one. She was their own Madame Albani. And Georgina was to cast the first and lasting impression of their otherwise upstanding village to all the people of the province. When chance visitors stopped by, they inevitably asked about their "star." But any desire to stop by and visit her was quickly squelched. "No, she doesn't accept visitors. She's, how shall we say, a little queer."

This wasn't strictly true. Georgina had visitors often. Musical people with pretentious hats would swoop down the main street of Stirling every now and again, crates of goodness-knows-what depravity piled in the boot of their carriages. And the first motor car that would grace Stirling would be that of a visitor of Georgina's.

After the last raspberry slice and lemon tart were eaten, after the teapot was emptied for the third time, the cream in the flowered Wedgwood jug much diminished, after the last goodbyes were said, Margaret donned her coat, buttoned her walking shoes, and set out for the lighthouse.

Again, the music was in the air. And though it was not sunny, the thick duvet of cloud was high enough not to obscure one's vision. As she neared Georgina's house, she was careful to keep her head straight on her shoulders and to glance only surreptitiously towards the sagging house set back off the road. She slowed her pace and put her ears at attention. There was music indeed. Only this time, Margaret was sure that the tones of a horn mingled with the rest. But she saw no movement behind the windows, no strangers on the porch. Nothing. Just the tall, dried stalks of the hollyhocks that Georgina had neglected to pull up when their flowering time was over.

Soon, she was so far past the house that she could no longer glance without turning her head and so she marched, her eyes fixed on the horizon, until she came to the lighthouse. There, she laid her hand on the cold plaster of the white tower, and sagged against it. Her heart was beating unbearably quickly, so quickly that her knees felt loose and unable to hold her weight. And there was an ache. The unnameable ache that accompanied her terrible dreams.

The high note of a voice, distinctly Georgina's, wafted to Margaret's resting place on a scrap of breeze. Margaret pulled herself upright and without glancing out to sea, walked straight home. But what she would do when she got there, she didn't know.

Margaret awoke the following morning with her damp nightgown twisted tightly around her waist. There had been three of them: laughing in the waves, flicking water at one another with their tails; floating, their breasts globes of light in the salty water. And when they saw her, the mermaids had beckoned her to the water's edge with their singing, high and trilling.

Margaret set her teeth. Instead of letting the dream haunt her, inhabit the corners of her mind throughout the day, she expelled it with ferocity. Today, she, Mrs. Margaret Hawkins, would set that Georgina straight, though she had no idea what she'd do. The woman had gone too far, disrupting the lives of decent people. Margaret began her morning chores of washing up, chopping kindling and polishing the door knobs and banisters clean of fishy fingerprints.

When all was as it should be, Margaret slipped on her gloves, took her shawl from the hook by the icebox and shut the door of her house behind her. The streets of Stirling were empty yet, the children at school and the women scrubbing away winter's greyness. Only the McDaniels' dog, an ugly curr with one flopping ear, took note of Margaret. When she paid its wagging tail no attention, it followed its nose into the bushes. By now, it was truly spring; the flowers were in blossom and the cemetery trees were in full leaf. Soon the lilacs would bloom. Lilacs were her favourite.

Where the road forked, one branch leading to the churchyard, the other to the lighthouse point, Margaret paused. It would have been good to forget this thing, be done with it, to have banished it from her thoughts long ago. But that had not transpired. She filled her lungs with purposeful air and set out with her quick, long stride. Soon — too soon — she was in front of Georgina's house and felt her earlier resolve waver. She slowed her steps as the strains of a tune caught her attention. Strings again. And a voice — no, two — Georgina's own above that of another woman.

Georgina's window was open a sliver as if to let morsels of music slip out. It was as if she was taunting Margaret. And through this very same open window a thin, genie wisp of grey smoke slipped out, wafting upwards and dissipating in the breeze. The air stilled for a moment and the next wisp of smoke flowed down the peeling clapboard and advanced across the greening grass like a cat gingerly testing the earth. It crept across the yard towards the road where its acrid scent caught in Margaret's nostrils.

Margaret suddenly realized that she was standing in the middle of the road staring unabashedly at Georgina's house.

No. No. I will walk to the point, Margaret told herself. *To the lighthouse. That's all.* But by the time she reached the lighthouse, she still had not decided what to do. Knock on the door? And say what? It would not do to let Georgina catch her tongue-tied. Perhaps she could invite her to the sewing bee ... No. What if she decided to come? Perhaps she could ask for a donation to the missionary fund. It was everyone's duty to assist the heathen. Her mind made up, Margaret walked to Georgina's house, to Georgina's door, her hand poised to knock, without hesitation.

As she mounted the walk, the music grew louder, more clear. She lifted her hand to knock and one of the instruments inside sawed low and sweet, fiddles chirped and the bass thrummed. Before she could stop herself, Margaret's hand was on the door-knob, not raised to knock the flat, dumb wood, but curled around the cool of the knob. And before she knew what she was doing, she turned it and pushed.

The door careened open, wide.

Inside, Georgina whirled to face Margaret, her lips parted not with song but with astonishment. Margaret noticed that Georgina's dark hair hung loosely to her waist and tendrils curled, uncombed, on the soft plane of her cheek. Her full lips seemed so red, searing red against the background of her pale, heart-shaped face. And her eyes ...

Georgina's vulnerable gaze held Margaret's. The sweet saw-ing of the music enveloped them, the violins soaring, the melody and Georgina's soft green eyes burning themselves into Margaret's memory. She did not know how long they stood there, eyes locked, until Margaret finally cast her glance around the small living room. It was empty of people.

"But the music ..." Margaret uttered.

Flustered by the words, Georgina turned away suddenly, knocking against the small table from where the music seemed to emanate. The music screeched to a dreadful halt. A large brass horn fell, clattering across the table. Something shattered, and shards of black disk rained across the floor.

"My gramophone!" Georgina cried out, falling to her knees among the black pieces. "My Chopin!"

Margaret wished she could run. She wished she could close the door as though it had never been opened but her feet riveted her to the doorstep. The silence immobilized her. Her heart pounded, and in her head, confusion thundered.

Finally, Georgina looked up, her face suddenly grey and thin, her hair limp and lusterless. The astonishment in her eyes had turned to fear. "Why do you hate me so?" Georgina uttered, almost as if to herself.

And Margaret could think of nothing to say, no excuse, no apology, nothing. Her arms rose, extended themselves towards Georgina, in spite of herself. In her throat, in her chest, an ache. Only an ache.

The River

KAREN HANLON

THE RIVER was the highest it had been for twenty-three years. Frenzied and demented, its muddy water rushed downstream, forming vortexes around tree trunks and bushes. Many objects slanted and jumped in the current; old logs, pieces of fence, garbage and — most horrible and compelling of all — a bloated animal's carcass would occasionally appear, obscene and ravaged in the tumult.

Shelagh sat in her housecoat, by herself at the kitchen window, staring deeply into the water's madness. She spoke to the air, "Lamb of God ... Lamb of God, who taketh away the sins of the world, have mercy upon me ... Lamb of God, now and at the hour of my death, grant me peace."

Absently the words fell out of her mouth. Her eyes, normally squinted with the first signs of middle age, were wide and unfocused, her vision distorted. The water, stretched over half her lawn, lapping against the raised perennial garden barely fifty feet from the house. Each spring it was the same, she thought, the freshet came in its disquieting way spilling over the grassy banks of their narrow southern New Brunswick river, covering the tree roots along the shore and shortening the fields of the farm on the opposite side. But this year was different, the thaw had come quick and wet and the water had never before been this close to her door. Today, for the ninth day in a row, the rain fell against her window.

His voice summoned her back to the kitchen. "Shelagh," he was yelling from the top of the stairs. "Shelagh, the kids aren't up and its nearly seven o'clock. What are you doing?"

"Auugh," she scowled and got off the window seat. "I'm making breakfast. You call them, you're closer." They had argued the night before because she'd allowed Jason, their oldest son, to take the truck and not told him what time to be home.

One by one, showered and half-asleep, her four teenaged sons joined her. She dished hot oatmeal into their bowls. Mac hustled in, his large hands awkwardly stuffing papers into his laptop computer case. Shelagh held the pot of porridge up in his direction. He looked down from his six-foot-five-inch altitude; the wall of anger was still fixed in each of their gazes. "I'll get a coffee later," he said and turned to the boys. "Get your things ready, I'll give you a ride to school. The water's too high to walk."

Shelagh audibly exhaled. It was something she couldn't figure out. This was Mac's river; from the time he was a boy he'd claimed it for his own, and made sure that his sons were brought up beside it too. A thousand times, it seemed, she'd heard him laughing, telling about the raft he and his sister had built to race against the neighbour kids in the spring current. "The trick," he would say, his voice filled with excitement, "was to lie flat and push yourself clear of obstacles with a pole, and if you got knocked off, to grab like hell onto anything you could find." Yet, whenever the boys were on the riverbank, he stood at the window. And even in the summer, seventeen-year-old Jason wasn't allowed to take the canoe out by himself. He constantly lectured them on water safety but always forgot to wear his own life jacket.

She had a picture of him as she imagined he'd been on that raft, a tall boy with light brown hair hanging in his eyes, stretched out over the planks, fearless and laughing as he careened down the river. That's the way he'd been when they'd first met at the University of Calgary, a big mad "Maritimer" ready to do anything. Their friends said they'd both end up dead the way they fed on each other's daring. Every weekend they went off heli-skiing, or repelling down mountain faces, exploring caves, anything one could think of they both would do. The first time he'd said he loved her he was driving on sheer ice down a twelve-percent grade and she was laughing as he turned the car out of a slew. That Mac, she thought, would have been out building rafts with his sons, not driving them past the river so they wouldn't get too close to the edge.

The phone rang as she was dressing for work. Shelagh followed the noise into Jason's bedroom, where she found the portable under a pair of discarded jeans.

"Is this Mrs. Malcolm Gallagher at Sixty-one Strand Road?"

An instant weight pulled painfully on the left side of her chest. She knew immediately it was about Mac and the boys.

"Yes," she said.

A male voice spoke mechanically, "This is Greg Valence of the Emergency Measures Organization, Mrs. Gallager." He paused. She grabbed hold of the bedpost to steady herself. "I don't want to alarm you, but we are making the residents in your neighbourhood aware that the ice appears to be jamming, at the bridge, about a mile downriver from your property. If the jam does occur, your house is one that we are concerned may suffer flooding."

It took a while for her to grasp what he was saying. Her pounding heart and dry throat were attached to her fear for Mac and the boys, not to the house. Then she realized she'd been mistaken and relief made what he'd told her seem unimportant. After all, she thought, when you're a prairie farmer's daughter you know that you can't expect to go through life without any trouble at all.

She dealt offhandedly with him, "I'll be at work until two this afternoon. Can I give you my number there so you can inform me if anything definite happens?"

"Well, yes, ma'am. Certainly," he replied, "but you do realize what with the jamming and the amount of rain forecast for the next couple of days, the water levels are apt to rise very quickly?"

His condescending tone told her that this was a serious situation, and that he thought she was a fool. Embarrassed, she cleared her throat and asked, "What would you suggest I do?"

He told her to pack her clothes, move any property she could to higher ground, and that if it became necessary to evacuate the house her phone would begin ringing in a short continuous sequence. Should this happen, she was to leave immediately.

At the end of the hall she opened the window, and leaned out to her waist holding onto the frame with one hand in an effort to see downstream to the bridge. The rain and wind hit hard against her and the noise from the river banged into her ears. Beyond the neighbour's trees, she could make out the bend where ice chunks and debris were slamming and piling together. Below, puffs of fog danced and chased each other in the air. She saw the water on her lawn and wondered if it had risen since she'd last looked. At the corner of the verandah a piece of loose trim caught in the gale was being battered backwards until it was nearly broken in two.

This old house, with its tall windows and square walls, had always stood solid against any weather. Mac had wanted to own it since he was a child. When they were first married, and living in the city, he would take her by canoe, from upriver at his mother's place, and paddle back and forth in front of the Victorian mansion. "That's the place to raise kids," he'd tell her. Then, when miraculously — for Mac had thought of it as a miracle — it came up for sale, they'd borrowed more money than they could afford and bought it. Jason had been a baby and she was pregnant with Mark when they'd moved in. Within the following three years, Mick and Scott were added, and as the boys grew, the house and its three acres of property had provided them with the sturdiness and space they needed. Inside these strong walls she'd always looked down at the river as a feudal lord might look at a comely tenant. And even now, after the stern warning she'd just received, she couldn't conceive that their grassy-banked river had the power to harm such a stronghold.

Going back inside, she tried to decide what to do about work. It was Monday, the pharmacy would be busy and she had a shipment to unpack in the afternoon. Would her boss consider a river threatening to invade her walls reason enough to stay home? She decided to call Mac.

It took five minutes to get through the switchboard at the paper mill and ten more before they were able to track him down. He was a supervisory engineer and his job took him all over the plant. "Shelagh, what's up?" he said casually when he answered, but in his voice she could hear his irritation at being disturbed.

"Were you busy?"

"Yes."

She told him her message, and it came as a surprise when he said without hesitation that he would be right home. The head pharmacist too showed only solicitude when she finally called to say that she wouldn't be in.

Driven by restlessness she went down to the cellar. There, under one bare light bulb, boxes of every description lined the stone walls. All were neatly labelled: Christmas ornaments, camping gear, tapes, records. Obscure and seldom used things, they stared at her from the plywood shelves appealing to be rescued. She began lugging them up three flights of stairs to the attic. At the window on the second-floor landing she could look down to the river, but the rain obstructed her view and it was hard to tell if the water was getting higher.

On her fourteenth trip, the box of school scrapbooks and the one that read "Hockey Memorabilia" had seemed perfectly manageable when she'd started off with them, but by the time she reached the front hall the two were precariously balancing in an increasingly uneven shift. Then as she rounded the newel post the front door opened, causing her to jump, and the records of her husband's youthful prowess spilled at his feet. From his great height, rain dripping off his hair and khaki jacket, he looked down at the team pictures and newspaper clippings scattered about him, and knelt to pick them up. Shelagh was already doing the same.

"Shelagh, you pick the oddest times to house clean," he said.

"I was worried about fire," she replied, and he smiled somewhat distractedly.

"What are you doing with this stuff?"

"Taking it to the attic along with the other boxes in the basement."

She heard him release a long breath, and noted that his knuckles were white on the scrapbook he was gripping. "That basement's never had water in it in the hundred years it's been here," he said through his teeth. "It's got to be that goddamned new bridge. Those fool architects should have known; the way the ice breaks up in this river it couldn't get past that centre abutment. Serve them right if the whole bridge goes out with the ice." The anger wreaked raw in his voice and Shelagh placed her hand on his arm.

"What do they care if people's houses get destroyed?" he continued. "They'll just deny it had anything to do with the bridge, and declare this area a flood plain so not even the damned insurance will be any good. And all of us up in Fredericton last year tellin' them this would happen. Bloody stupid arses." His voice remained loud and scornful, but where their limbs touched Shelagh could feel the trembling in him.

"Mac, a little water in the basement won't destroy the house," she reasoned quietly.

He lifted his eyes from the floor and looked at her with contempt. Shrugging her arms away he said, "You don't know what you're talking about, Shelagh. I'm going to go call Mom, to tell her to pick up the boys after school and take them to her place."

Always he did this to her, excluded her because she'd grown up on the prairies and wasn't native to his precious rural New Brunswick. It didn't matter to him that she'd lived here nearly half her life, for so long that all that clearly remained to her of the West was the colours of the Chinook arcing across the sky, and the taste of its warm sweet air filling her brittle lungs. To Mac she was still someone foreign, someone who didn't understand, and it was little comfort to know that he was right. Outside, the wind was gaining strength, jarring the windows, vibrating through the house; Shelagh felt it rattle the empty spaces inside her, and drew her sweater tight at the neck.

A few minutes later, Mac was back asking her to help him drain the pipes, seal the doors and windows and move whatever they could to the upper stories. She thought their time would be better spent in getting sand and bags to build a barricade around the house; but she said nothing and did what he asked. At noon the river was another two feet closer to the house. Somewhere the ice broke a hydro pole and they lost their power.

Two strangers from the E.M.O., in green rain gear with orange reflector cross vests, came to the door and said that the water was over the road by the bridge and that their section of the village had been closed. They gave Mac a pass to get in and out of the road blocks, and told him that he should move the car and truck to higher ground. Inside the rubber hoods, Shelagh noted that their faces were flushed with heat and drenched with rain. The younger man asked her if she had their suitcases packed in case they had to leave quickly. Why don't you ask Mac if he's packed the clothes, she thought with indignation. Ignoring him, she asked his partner if the river had blocked yet.

"It's closed off enough so that we can expect the worst," he replied. "The flow on the other side of the bridge is only a fraction of what it was yesterday, and on this side there is six hundred cubic meters of water a second bearing down on the ice build up. I'm afraid that unless it breaks soon there'll be bad flooding."

Sitting on the bare window seat, his big frame leaning forward with his elbows resting on his knees, Mac contrived to give the impression that he presided over the room. There was no trace left of the anguish that had been in his voice when he'd come home that morning. They spoke together leisurely, as if discussing last night's hockey game. The E.M.O. men told how the ice was piled up ten feet high at the bridge and that six "flat beds" loaded with potash had been moved onto the span to help secure it against being washed away. They warned them that wells were being monitored for contamination, but tests took time and it wasn't a good idea to drink the tap water.

They were interrupted by the phone ringing, which reminded their visitors that they had to leave. She could hear Mac arguing with Jason as the E.M.O. officers gave her their final instructions, warning her that they should be prepared to evacuate at any time. As they left, Mac held up a hand to them and Shelagh held the door against the wind to keep It from banging into the wall.

"It's not possible, son, the roads are closed. You couldn't do anything anyway." Mac's voice was firm, but Jason was obviously having none of it. "No, Jason, listen, the water is rising quickly; your mother and I could have to leave any minute now ... I don't know how high it is ... I don't know. Look I want you to find Mark and tell him that Gram is picking you both up after school." His eyes met Shelagh's with an expression of exasperation.

"Listen to me, Jason. You can't get to this side of the river now without going all the way to the bridge at Culter. Just tell me what you want and I'll bring it for you ... I don't know, maybe thirty feet from the house." He stood with one hand splayed on the wall, silently listening for a minute and then spoke again. This time his willed control was audible and he averted his gaze from her. "Where did you leave it? ... Who else has been with you in this?" She saw the colour drain from his face as Jason answered. "I hope you know that you could have killed them all. Tell me exactly where you tied it last ... Go home with your grandmother," he said and hung up.

"They've been taking the canoe out in that," he answered her puzzled face and made a gesture with his hand towards the river. "What do you think they were trying to do, commit suicide?"

"Oh, my God," was all she could answer.

"They have it tied in the trees on the other side of the raspberries. I better go see if I can get it." He sounded as if he was only half aware of what he was saying.

"You should take a rope," she said. "I'll go get the one in the cellar."

Halfway down the steps her flashlight beam reached the bottom and reflected back something shiny. Confused, she shone the light farther only to discover that the entire earthen floor had become luminous, and finally upon reaching the bottom step, Shelagh realized that it was water. Involuntarily, her hand shook the flashlight, and then everything about the flood became real to her. This river, that her husband loved, in whose bosom they'd taught their sons to swim, did not love them. It was indifferent and Godless, and would have no qualms about destroying the foundation of her home or leaving mud, filth, mold, and rot in its wake. She stood frozen on the staircase overpowered by her own helplessness and weak with anger. Somewhere upstairs, she was dimly aware, a sound like a fire bell began and didn't stop.

"Shelagh." It was Mac's voice. "Shelagh, that's the evacuation ring. We've got to go. Come on. I've got the clothes."

It was his urgency, rather than his words, that penetrated

through her stupor and jolted her back to her senses. Overhead on the wall she saw the rope she'd been after and remembered the canoe. No ... the word came to her viscerally, no ... She could practically feel it singeing her flesh. Quickly she took down the rope and raced back up the stairs. Mac wasn't there. The shrill short blasts of the phone were too loud to bear. Grabbing her raincoat she made her way out the door. Her husband was at the car putting the suitcases in the trunk. He saw her and threw her the keys, "Where've you been? Here, take the truck; it's higher and better able to get through water."

She came up to him, her small figure standing squarely under his great height.

"I'm getting the canoe first," she said.

He tried to argue, to make her see sense. He told her that the water was rising quickly, and the roads could be blocked if they delayed. He said the boys would be looking for them. None of it moved her.

"There's water in the cellar," she said and started walking to the other side of the house.

As she turned the corner, she had a glimpse of Mac standing by the open car door. She picked up here pace. "Go ahead and leave. See if I care," she shouted at him inside her head. The water was noticeably higher than it had been even a few minutes before. She walked bent at the waist navigating Into the wind and rain towards the raspberries. The freshet now reached into the lower end of the berries, deep enough so that only a few branches breached its crests. She forged a path through the top of the patch to a sheltered stand of soft wood. Here in the lee of the wind it was somewhat quieter. She stood, her hands loosely clasping the coil of rope, turning it round and round with quick thrusts, and began to survey the water for some sign of the canoe. From behind a loud crack punctured the air. She swung around, with her heart nearly coming out of her chest, and saw Mac ten feet away with a tree branch snapped in two under his foot. For a few seconds she gaped at him, as if he were a mirage, then turned back to her task.

"Where did he say they tied it?" she asked.

"Down there." He pointed to where the river was ripping through a cluster of birch. Straining her eyes she tried to make out the form of the boat or glimpse its green against the brown and white landscape.

"I can't see it," she said. "Are you sure it was there he meant?"

"The far side of the raspberries, in the trees, by the lower end of the patch. It could have gone adrift, or sunk." His voice was gentle, but he stood, with his brow creased, impatiently shifting from foot to foot.

Shelagh gave no sign of noticing. "We should be able to see the rope at least," she said, craning her neck and pacing along the edge of the water. Her hood had blown off and her hair hung in stringy rivulets. She didn't bother to wipe the rain from her face. Downriver, the ice that eddied here in the whirlpools continued to crash together sending its dissonant thunder blasting back to their ears. She wished she could see deeper into the mess in front of her. A few feet out in the water she noticed a mature apple tree that looked as if it would be easy to climb. In desperation she considered reaching it, but she knew it was a crazy idea. There were large branches out there being sucked under in the current. What chance would she have of keeping her footing? For another moment she searched as far as she could see into the trees and even in that short time the rising water lapped over the toes of her boots. Setting her jaw she turned around and faced her husband.

"Damn," she said. "I wanted to save it." A sigh of resignation escaped from her lips. "I suppose we'd better go." He remained dumb, but his eyes were soft and his answer laid in his twisted smile.

The wind was behind them on their return trek making it

easier to walk, keeping their faces dry and allowing them respite to take in the altered vista. It was like being in an incoherent dream. There was no horizon, only an indefinable foggy sky that either hung down to the ground, or lifted up past the treetops and was littered with pieces of broken clouds that whipped by in lost and aimless frenzy. The flower gardens and bushes were gone, the dock too, obliterated by the dark riled water that swallowed everything familiar and left only the tops of the blue spruces eerily sticking out of its surface. They walked close together to steady each other over the slippery patches, moving quickly trying to recapture some of the time they'd lost.

In front of the wisteria, by the verandah, Shelagh snagged her boot on a rock and felt herself begin to pummel forward. The instant before her face hit the brambles she managed to fling out her hand and grab Mac's sleeve. Alerted by the tug of her weight, he instinctively reached around and pulled her against his chest.

"Woa darlin'," he said. "Watch the shrubbery or you'll be lowering the property value."

It was their own quirky brand of humour and its familiarity in the midst of this surreal day acted as balm to her taut nerves. But it was short-lived, as quickly as he'd saved her he let her go, and they moved on.

And then, when they did at last get to the vehicles it was Mac who couldn't leave. He had to rush to lock the doors and look through the windows, until Shelagh insisted they go. When he was finally in the car behind her, she put the truck in gear and drove up the driveway and onto the road. She kept her eyes focused ahead out the windshield, willing herself not to look back at what they'd forsaken. Her body seemed heavy as the weariness of exhaustion and the heat of the truck began to settle in. A part of her wanted to weep, but mostly she wished for sleep. It came into her mind, how the Jews believed that in death you lost your sense of self and became a speck in the light of God: ever in rapture, ever free of pain, ever at peace, ever numb,

The River

ever blessed. The empty road wound ahead of her, ten miles up river to the Culter bridge and eight back to her mother-in-law's house. There were no other vehicles, no errant water: just the slip-slap of windshield wipers, the force of the wind making the steering wheel dance, and the faint yellow glow of Mac's fog lights in her rear-view mirror.

The Years of the Strawberry Circus

Emily Schultz

THE FIRST TIME I met Josh, he was talking about self-love — masturbation really. And isn't it just a form of narcissism? Don't most women fantasize by looking in the mirror? The way Josh said it, it wasn't much of a question.

Brenda went on to talk about using her pillow and her stuffed bear, Miriam closed her eyes as if she was going to throw up, and this hippie guy muttered that the problem with masturbation was that you could never kiss your own mouth. But conversations like that happened all the time, in bars or on street corners and after a while the colours of passing people and the strains of their voices blurred together. Josh was just background.

But he kept popping up. The first time after that, I think, was on the bus and it was raining. The smells of people sitting so close had gotten mixed up the way they do: sweat and newsprint, coffee steam from paper cups, hairspray, overdone aftershave, a whiff of rubber boots, urine, basement. Wet, restless, excited. I didn't notice he was there until he pulled the cord and stood up. He zipped up his jacket and jumped out into the pissy rain without my having to say hi. The bus lurched past him, and the day moved on, into other days.

I was still living with Miriam then. Here in Windsor, of course.

The Years of the Strawberry Circus

On South Street, just a block behind the Chippewa Tavern. Remember a few years back, that couple on trial for killing their baby? They used to live just a block up, on Peter. So you get the idea. Our whole neighbourhood was depressing. Even three-year-olds would teeter out onto their porches to tell us to fuck off. We rode the bus a lot, me and Miriam. Neither one of us could afford a car. Miriam changed jobs from week to week and I mostly borrowed from my parents. We pretended to be high school girls so we could get a student bus rate, and on week-ends, or particularly grungy afternoons we went drinking downtown. On one or two Saturday nights at places with bands and cover charges, Miriam promised she'd go down on the door guy, and we ducked in for free, and out again before last call, before he could try to collect. But at our regular bars, they got to know our faces, and we didn't have to bring our ID. We always wore jeans and when skinny bar girls in dresses walked by, Miriam would turn to me and say, Let them eat cake. Then we would try to get everyone in the bar jigging, if it happened to be a pseudo-Irish band, and if it wasn't, we would sit in the corner and talk about love because we didn't have any. Or the politics of sister-hood, if it happened to be a particularly bad night. Or sometimes someone we knew would offer to share some pot with us in the alley, and then my hair would become a living thing on my head, little lights at the tips of strands, which tickled when I touched them. That was where we were coming from — where I was coming from.

And in the day I ran into him on the street. All the time I started seeing him. He worked at a downtown restaurant, the kind appealing to Casino tourists and American businessmen, its patio extending into the sidewalk. As I was carousing with Miriam, or running meagre errands alone, he would be shouldering trays the size of tables, food to feed armies of businessmen. He would glide out over the railing with forty pounds balanced on a shoulder no wider than mine, and never miss a beat, sweep the whole load down in one motion, dishes delicately placed by some other sudden hand. And somehow, he always noticed me passing by and found the breath midsweep for an unbroken hello.

You have to say hello back in a situation like that. You're too awed to ignore it. I had to, anyway. Miriam didn't remember ever meeting him, even after I reminded her. Oh, she said, as though it had happened to someone else. I remembered because I had seen him so often since, but also because the pieces didn't match up.

The day that Miriam left for Toronto, we took a cab downtown to the train station. She had a suitcase and an old hockey bag of her brother's. She wasn't taking any furniture. It was all from yard sales and wasn't worth the trouble. We weren't late and we probably could have managed the stuff on the bus, but we took the cab anyway. It felt like we should do something different, something to remind ourselves before it happened.

We stood in line and bought her ticket together. I owed her money for the groceries that were still sitting in the fridge. We had twenty minutes until her train, and we spent it reading the personals to each other, laughing at how people define themselves.

Then she stood up and hoisted her bags all around her so I couldn't hug her. Unless she initiated it, Miriam was opposed to contact. She had endured it once or twice from me, always stiffening and retreating quickly. Well, I hate goodbyes, she said, shifting her weight from foot to foot.

See you later, I said.

Yeah, see you.

She turned to walk away to put her things on the train, and I didn't hug her. I let her go, watching the back of her head, I thought about how fast her hair had grown and how the next time I saw her she would have it long enough to pull back.

The Years of the Strawberry Circus

She called a couple days later. She had left some things behind, things she needed right away, she said. They were mostly odds and ends: thick-framed sunglasses, a cup, a book of scraggly cat drawings, a few magazines, and homemade tapes, the pair of scissors with the green handles, and she'd decided she wanted the kitchen clock after all. The clock had a picture of Strawberry Shortcake on its face, and as I pulled it down I noticed the orange brush strokes all around the outside. Miriam had left it up and painted around it. I found the other things on her shelves or in her chest of drawers. Our stuff had gotten mixed up after three years together. I had been missing the cassettes for some time. The scissors were mine too. I put them in the box with the other things and mailed them to her.

A couple months later, I quit scamming student loans for the college classes I never attended. I took a full-time job waitressing. I thought of him sometimes at the end of shifts that had been busiest. It bothered me that I couldn't remember his name, especially after he'd said hello so many times. But more than that, I thought about what kind of person it takes to say hello to an almost-stranger in the middle of rush hour with forty pounds of dishes hovering overhead. I hadn't seen him in a long time, he must have quit the job at the restaurant downtown.

Miriam called sometimes. She had become quite the bar bunny though, and kept a lot of boys coming and going at her whim, so I didn't call her much — it always seemed to be an inappropriate moment. I wondered how she got away with the things she got away with. She found ways to meet boys no matter where she was — at night at concerts, and in the day at the post office, the subway station, the falafel hut. It wasn't her fault, she said, I wasn't around to keep her in line. Toronto was huge without me, and when was I coming anyway?

I didn't have an answer for that one, and she knew better than to ask twice. There was nothing really holding me to this town. Nothing but the rent and the lease, my unexplainable attachment to the chimney-sweep flavour of Windsor's characters. But none of that has any hold really. Money, promises, love. There are ways to forget about those things. They were excuses and Miriam knew it.

This town is swallowing us whole, she said to me the night she decided to leave. She didn't say it again.

I finally went to see her in Toronto. She had gotten herself into some drama program there. I could have visited her before. I had lots of friends who wouldn't have minded a weekend road trip, or wanted someone to split the gas money. But whenever I wasn't working, Miriam had exams or auditions, and when she finished those, I was working again. That was an excuse too, and I knew it even at the time. Even after I found a replacement roommate, in my head it was still Miriam's Room. As much as she wanted me to join her in Toronto, I wanted her to come back here.

Nights when I was way too drunk I called her from the bar and left long messages on her answering machine. I can't remember what I said, probably nothing, but I remember holding myself in bed afterwards, unable to move my legs, and thinking, if I have to throw up I won't even be able to get out of bed. Then I would start to shake, believing I must have alcohol poisoning and if only Miriam were still living here, she would know what to do. I'm going to die, I thought. I'm going to die, I'm going to die.

Miriam left messages too, but even stoned or depressed she seemed whimsical. Oh, she said into the machine, It's raining today and I'm all out of oranges and that really made me sad so I thought I would call and now you aren't home either. I bought a whole bunch of Clementines last week and they were so perfect and today I didn't have any money for lunch, so I was looking forward to getting home and eating oranges and drinking this fabulous licorice-root tea I got. But I forgot I ate the last ones a couple nights ago, in bed with this stupid intellectual boy I brought home. He had a goatee and I know you're cringing and saying, a goatee? but he had a huge bag of weed and he wanted to talk about Foucault, and at the time it seemed so exciting. Now it just seems smarmy and pathetic. Foucault, Derrida. Oh so much for my week. I'm just babbling. You have to call me back and tell me something real.

After weeks of one-sided conversations I was surprised when she actually picked up.

Miriam? I asked her.

Yeah, who else would it be?

Fuck, I told her. That's it.

And I gave in and bought the ticket the next day.

She had class when my bus got in so I spent the afternoon knocking around the shops on Queen. But honestly, the dollar stores all down Yonge were more my style. We had agreed to meet at a coffee shop. I found the place easily, about thirty minutes early. I read a freebie paper.

Love is love is love, my horoscope scolded me. You have been hiding your feelings from yourself. You will find consequences quietly kept in drawers among the forks.

I saw Miriam before she saw me. She was standing kitty-corner to me, among six or seven other people waiting to cross. She was wearing a green and white polkadot scarf over her hair, and the thick-framed sunglasses I had mailed back to her. A pink raincoat and red lipstick. She looked like a 1950s movie star between February's black and grey hats and coats. The window was half steamed up and I saw the colour before I saw her face. Crossing the street, her steps seemed too long for her body, her hands thrust deep in her pockets, like she'd just as soon be anywhere.

I stood up when she came in, but she saw me as soon as her hand hit the door. Fancy running into you here, she said. She leaned over and kissed me on the cheek, leaving lipstick on me as if I was her boyfriend.

Her apartment was on Carleton and Jarvis, and turned out to be one room for living and sleeping. There was also a kitchen the size of a bathroom and a bathroom the size of a cubicle. She had rag-rolled the walls the colour of caramel corn and left masking tape running along the baseboards. A nail hole in the wall was the size of my thumb, evidence of poor plaster. So the Strawberry Shortcake clock had been hung by a string from the kitchen door handle. She had scattered bay leaves by the sink to combat cock-roaches. But it was something she didn't share with anyone else. The dishes were hers, the telephone was hers, the Klimt and Dali posters taped to the walls, the cupboards stocked with potatoes and peanut butter, the bathtub and blackberry bubble bath, the kitchen table in the middle of the living room — all hers.

She got self-conscious and began picking up the towels and clothes that were strewn from the bathroom to the bed.

I lived with you, I teased her.

Oh yeah, she said. She dumped the clothes into one pile in the corner. Well, what do you think, then?

It's beautiful, I told her.

We went out that night and got sloppy drunk with an armful of Miriam's friends. She excitedly introduced me to everyone: Carey, Michelle, Ella, and Slav. She joked with them like she had known them forever. I don't know what I had expected. She had this new life somewhere else and I was still in the same life she'd left me in. I took charge by filling everyone's glasses again and again.

Carey, the girl sitting next to me, asked me how Miriam and I had wound up as roommates. She kept stealing my boyfriends, I told her.

Carey looked like she didn't believe me. She asked if I was masochistic. Why would I ever move in with someone who stole my boys?

I figured we must have something in common, I confided.

She didn't understand. Didn't you date anyone? she wanted to know. Didn't you get lonely?

Not really. I lived with Miriam. What other entertainment could I need? Besides, I said, I learned to masturbate really, really well.

It was springtime when I saw him again. I had quit the job at the restaurant. It was raining again, after a long afternoon of hiking around with résumés and bad shoes. My hair was wet and hair-gel stringy and my feet were aching. It was just turning night. I walked towards this place with a green and white awning. I hadn't been there before but the sign above the door advertised the Corktown Criers with opening band Johnny Cum Lately. The place seemed too mom and pop for either band. Bar & Grille, an orange neon sign declared from the window.

When I walked in the tables were still cluttered from the dinner rush. He was there. He was carrying a grey plastic bus-bin, clanking spoons into cups, clattering knives onto plates.

He recognized me but couldn't place me right away. He wiped the tabletop in front of me, balancing the bin of dishes against his hip with his other arm. There was a beer bottle and I saw that it was going to topple. With restaurant-quick hands we both swiped for it. It deflected off my fingers and he caught it in his dishrag hand.

He set the bottle in the corner of the bin. He asked me if I was Miriam's friend. He said his name was Josh.

He mentioned Miriam's hair, how he remembered her because he used to be able to see her coming from halfway down the street. All that red hair.

I nodded. Before it got trendy she couldn't find dye that colour, and she used to use Kool-Aid. She would stain her lips with it too.

He set the bin on the bar and gathered clean glass ashtrays to glide onto the tables. That's right, he said, I remember the two of you looked completely mismatched next to each other. Like opposites. She always looked like she was on some nasty trip, and you, well, you look like you haven't gone yet.

Hey, I protested, I'm not that naive.

Oh, I don't mean it that way. I don't mean it that way at all.

He didn't tell me what he did mean. And I didn't ask. He was humming two stray lines of a pop song over and over, and I decided there were worse places to be. Josh poured me another coffee, heavy on the Irish Cream. He didn't charge me. I wondered if it was an apology.

It felt good to sit in on the in-between stuff. He was so casual it made me feel welcome, like I came in every day for that coffee, or like I worked there too. He moved around the room like he owned it, swinging chairs into place, clunking their wooden legs against each other. He had the place in order before I could even start the second drink.

Johnny Cum Lately got there late, a bunch of high school boys in plaid pants. A lot of safety pins. I thought they might have something intelligent to sing, but it turned out they just wanted to be rock stars. I had seen Corktown Criers several times before with Miriam. They were from Detroit, with put-on accents. Maybe the singer had an Irish grandfather. But it didn't matter. They knew how to make some danceable noise. And more and more people were drawn in. I finished my second, then my third Irish Cream, and ordered a pint. I watched the bar fill up.

A girl with Raggedy Ann braids was hopping up and down in front of the blasting speaker, flopping her head from side to side. She had a Guinness in one hand and her other arm across the shoulder of another girl, a shadow thrown from her. They were moving together, laughing under the spotlight, the Raggedy Ann girl's mouth open and red, her eyes wild. Fuck it, she was saying, laughing. Fuck it. This is it.

The Years of the Strawberry Circus

Josh picked up my empty pint glass. Dark or pale ale, he wanted to know.

That girl, I said in his ear, pointing and gripping his forearm. That girl.

He looked confused, followed my finger. Yeah? he asked.

She looks like my friend.

Yeah, he said. Yeah she does. Wherever you go there's always someone like her.

No, I told him. There isn't.

No, he said. He could only half-hear me, and he was distracted, trying to get the drink orders and collect the empties. He asked me if I wanted anything.

I want to go dance with her, I said, still clutching his shirtsleeve.

Okay, you go dance with her.

No. She's gone, you know.

Josh nodded and twisted away from the table into the crowd looking for other drink orders. He came back a few songs later. He brought me a coffee without any liqueur. I had been discreetly cut off.

He set it down in front of me. Wherever you go, you see those people around, he said, because you take them with you. He touched my shoulder and moved away.

I didn't see either Josh or Miriam again while I lived on South Street. Of course I would have seen her at Easter, but she had strep throat and didn't want to bus home. A friend from high school, Andrew, had opened a sandwich shop in the east end, and promised me as many hours as I wanted. I was ready to call it quits with the replacement roommates I'd had since Miriam. A place in the east end would be quiet, a balcony-sized step up, especially from South Street. I found that if I quit going out at night, somehow it was enough for a decent apartment. I didn't know what to do with the bulky pink davenport or the fake-wood end tables she had lugged home from the Goodwill. Even though I had used them more than she had, I felt like I was cleaning up after her.

Throw them out, she said when I called and asked her. She said she was going to Ireland. What? When? I had talked to her just a couple weeks before.

Oh love, can't you just see me there? We're talking a culture that has deified wide-hipped women and beer! Imagine me jigging to the real stuff and drinking with the people. I'm going to hitchhike across the entire country and back.

But how are you getting there? I asked.

It's this boy, she said. He and his girlfriend broke up so he has an extra ticket. One way.

Well, how would you get back? I asked.

She didn't answer.

I left her couch and tables in the apartment for the landlord. I wanted someone to clean up after me for once.

When you move into a new place, it's hard to think of it as yours. You have to decide where to put the furniture, the pictures, clock, and the hook for the colander. In my new apartment there wasn't a nail hole that hadn't been puttied and painted over. There wasn't any history, and I hadn't brought much with me.

I ate at the sandwich shop every day. Even in the beginning we had some okay times there. Me and my friend Andrew and his girlfriend Lynn. Lynn and I liked to gang up on Andrew. We teased him all day and he would act dejected, knocking the mop handle noisily against the booths. But by nighttime, I would be mopping, knocking around, while the two of them were laughing in the kitchen.

How can you not like mayonnaise? I would hear Lynn ask

him, and the threatening sound of the lid being unscrewed. Yummy, she would say, and I would hear him gagging. I could imagine her licking a gloppy spoonful of it to disgust him, or jamming it towards him. In some ways they always seemed like friends instead of a couple, the way Miriam and I always seemed like a couple instead of friends.

Miriam never did go to Ireland. The boy and his girlfriend got back together before the departure date. Miriam called me up at the restaurant in the middle of the day.

I'm moving to Espanola, she said.

Is that in New Mexico?

No, Ontario. It's a little town near Sudbury.

What's wrong with Toronto?

It's Toronto, she said, and I could almost hear her tossing her candy-apple head.

Well, what's in Espanola?

I don't know. What keeps you where you are? She sounded fed-up with me. If there's nothing to do, I'll just make something up. I think I'll be their town eccentric.

And that's what she did. I didn't ask her to come back and live with me, and she knew I wasn't going to follow her.

I got a photo from her in the mail maybe a half a year later. I don't remember her taking it. You can see the Strawberry Shortcake clock on the wall above me, and the map of the world pinned to the yellow refrigerator. I remember Miriam had drawn a big black X across the whole map and written YOU ARE HERE. In the picture, it doesn't show up, but I can see it anyway.

I'm standing at the counter, doing the dishes. She must have said my name to make me turn around so she could take the picture. My mouth is halfway open, like I was singing, or saying something to her. I look like I just woke up.

I took the picture and taped it to the fridge. It's a picture of me, but Miriam took it, so it's a picture of her too.

Finding Mother

JOANNE K. JEFFERSON

THE ROAD I drive on is an ordinary rural road, the same one our
school bus travelled. It always ended for us at our mailbox where
we met the seven trees lined along our lane. I can hear the
crunch of tires on the stones of the lane in my sleep sometimes,
dreaming my sister home from her job at the movie theatre, or
Uncle Harold with the wagon. But now I don't slow at the end of
that lane and turn the car into it, though the steering wheel
seems to want to pull me that way. I pass it with a long glance
over my shoulder, and continue on. To the nursing home.

The building sits back slightly from the road, on a small rise.
I turn in the driveway and follow the sign that tells me to park
around the back. The place is really an overgrown house with
several sections added on to what was once a well-proportioned
home, now institutionalized into awkwardness. Mother has a
room in the old part of the house and a window through which
she can see out to the bay and watch the tractors moving back
and forth across the fields of reclaimed salt marsh. She doesn't
remember the family guilt she used to express about those lands,
stolen six generations before her from the Acadian families who
had kept back the tides only to have some Protestant settlers
take their place.

I park the car, walk around the big pines that shelter the
north side of the house, climb the five wide steps, open the

heavy outside door that is locked only at night, wipe my feet on
the rough brown mat, and ring the small doorbell beside the
double glass doors with brass doorknobs. I watch the apparition
of the approaching Mrs. Lefort through the decorative cut glass,
her image split into a thousand smaller ones that are only parts
of her.

When I began visiting here, after Barbara and Uncle Harold
and I finally convinced Mother she couldn't stay home any
longer, Mrs. Lefort's place was an orderly relief from the chaos.
Now that the novelty is gone I try to amuse myself by looking for
something new or changed about the house and its decorations. I
have memorized Mrs. Lefort's entire wardrobe and the enormous
porcelain vase that stands on the mahogany table at the bottom
of the stairs and the grapevines carved in the oak bannister and
the landscape engravings hung on the wall of the upstairs hall.
Even Mother's room has stayed the same since she moved in.
The top of her dresser is covered by the same cross-stitched boy
and girl that she kept on it at home, their colours now faded with
age. As a child, I would stand on tiptoes in her room, stretching
to see the figures. I made up stories about the brother and sister
separated forever by the vast field of white. Sometimes I imagined I heard their tiny voices sending messages. Even here,
Grandma Laurence's silver brush and mirror set still rest on
the cloth.

I give Mother the cosmos I've brought. She always says the
same thing.

"Did you grow these yourself?"

"Yes," I say, choosing the half-truth since I don't have the
patience to explain, again, that I've been tending her garden all
summer, nurturing the perennials that Mother began setting out
when she and Dad first moved into the big house.

She puts the pink and purple blossoms with their feathery
leaves in her vase, the one that always stood on the top shelf of
the cabinet in the dining room. The cabinet with four wide

drawers in the bottom half and glass doors on the top. It was built right into the wall of the dining room and its wood was painted pale yellow. The round knobs on the glass doors were shiny black with brass screws in their centres. They always seemed to me, from my place across the dining-room table, like inside-out eyes.

Mother is living here because she can't seem to keep track of herself. We have no snappy title to attach to her loss of memory, her inability to decide whether to store the milk in the fridge or in the warming oven, her repeated accusation that the bank tellers were stealing from her safe-deposit box. We assumed it was symptoms of Alzheimer's, but the doctor tells us she is simply demented, a common enough condition for her age, and probably genetic.

She seems to have taken on a new persona to replace the lost one. The woman I visit frowns upon coarse language and boisterous laughter. She is critical and suspicious, especially of her new caregivers and the other inhabitants of this Home.

I miss the old Mother who would make terrible faces at me and tell the most hilarious stories about our neighbours, complete with accurate imitations of voice and manner. She sang alto in the church choir and was often asked by the organist to soften her attack; she was drowning out the sopranos. She loved to dance, and would swirl me around the kitchen when the lunch-hour radio played a reel. Perhaps it is her old self she speaks to so sharply as she looks in the full-length mirror on her closet door. I often come into her room to find her sitting in her chair, rocking at a brisk pace, lecturing her reflection.

I can barely stand these twice-weekly visits, the lagging conversations, the thousand repetitions of minor facts that seem to disappear as quickly as they are spoken. No, Joanie is twenty now and goes to college; no, the old barn burned in 1958; no, Elva Crouse lives down the hall here, since her husband died. We seem to cover the same territory each time, and make no progress. It is not about progress, I remind myself, only regress, as she goes farther away with each season. The worst days are those when I have to remind her of my name.

On one treasured afternoon of surprising clarity she told me a story I had never heard before about her mother. "I remember one day in winter," she said, "I must have been very young because Sarah was a tiny baby. Mama said, 'Oh, I don't want the coal man to bring the coal.' I asked her, 'Why, Mama?' And she said, 'Because we don't have the money to pay him.' My mother was proud and hated to owe money to anyone. Then we went out to the mailbox and there was a letter from Nana in England with two pounds in it. It would have taken three weeks or more to get to us. 'Mama,' I asked her, 'how did Nana know that we would need the money this day?' And she said 'God works in mysterious ways.' I remember her face so clearly." At the end of the story Mother was gone again and the rest of my visit was empty.

Right now the topic of choice is the climate. It is immediate and unsurprising.

"I find it terribly cold here," she tells me in a confiding tone, as if she doesn't wish to be caught complaining. "Do you need a sweater? I don't think they pay much attention to that sort of thing here. You know, I've asked them a hundred times to put more wood on, but it's always the same."

"I'll speak to Mrs. Lefort about that if you like, Mother," I tell her. I look out the window, distracted by a flock of birds that has settled on the power lines that stretch across the marsh and up the hill.

"Have you seen this photo?" Mother's voice returns me to awareness. "These are my grandchildren." She's right. It's a family shot of my sister Barbara and her husband, Ben, the Dean of Law, with their children Joan and Benjamin. In the picture the children are small, Benjamin a blond sprite at four, watching his older sister for clues. "She looks just like Ruth, don't you think?"

Mother asks, fingering the image of Joanie. "I've always been so proud of my Ruth."

I take the photo from her extended hand, seeing Barbara in the Ultrasuede suit she'd bought in Montreal, Ben in his tweed, the classics professor Barbara snagged instead of a degree at university. She'd settled her life into a hefty house on the river, a landscaper, a car of her own, and those children. Sweet children.

The last time Barbara and I spent any time together was the weekend in May when she came down from Fredericton in her Saab to help me clear out the house. We had finally agreed that it should be sold but before anyone could even make an appraisal it needed to be completely sanitized of its former life, freed from the mildew and grime that threatened to smother it. I spent the afternoon of that rainy Friday on my hands and knees in the upstairs bathroom and had gotten myself worked up to a resentful state, rehearsing all the complaints I would voice to Barbara when she arrived and saw what I had been dealing with. I imagined us eating takeout food at our old kitchen table amidst the dumped contents of Mother's kitchen drawers, but when Barbara breezed in, at five o'clock, she announced that she needed to ease herself after the long drive.

"I can't face this mess without a glass of wine and a meal with real silverware," she said. We went to town. Over dinner Barbara reminded me that I'd missed Benjamin's birthday.

"I'm not sure what that boy has planned, if anything," she sighed.

"He seems very committed to music," I offered.
Barbara looked at me over her glasses. "He's not like you, Ruth. He has no intention of studying formally or of choosing the stability of music education. You did the sensible thing."

And what has sensible done for me? I wondered silently. Barbara went on, "He auditioned for a band that's been playing the regional university circuit. I think they have a bagpiper or something. He's still waiting to hear back from them. He says he thinks they liked his original songs."

I made a mental note to send Benjamin the most encouraging card I could find, congratulate him on having the guts to try for it, and buy him a good set of strings.

"He's eighteen and he wants to spend his time hanging around in college bars, travelling and sleeping in a van with four others." She shuddered, the image apparently so far from her comfort level that she couldn't even bear the thought of someone else accepting it, even preferring it. "You never put yourself through any of that, Ruth. You served your community with your talents. Think of all those years you were church organist, and all those private lessons."

"Not much demand for violin players in rock bands twenty-five years ago." She didn't remember, or probably never knew about the few orchestra auditions I managed to get through: the cold sweat, the nausea, the blank mind once full of notes and bowing patterns.

We spent the rest of the evening at the house we'd grown up in, now nearly empty. Barbara sorted through the stacks of magazines and books while I scrubbed the walls. It wasn't until I was almost asleep, back in my own small house, listening to Barbara moving around my spare room, that I realized neither of us had spoken once of our shared childhood.

A quiet knock on the half-open door brings me back. It is Judith, one of the young women who works for Mrs. Lefort. "There's tea ready downstairs if you'd like some," she says. I put the photo back in its place on top of the dresser, beside Dad in his wedding suit, and me at my graduation. The pearl earrings, the brown hair, the serious eyes. I look up at Mother and see the same eyes.

"Maybe we should go down," I propose.

Mrs. Lefort's sitting room is heavy. That's the only way I can think to describe it. The drapes are heavy and even when they're pulled back they don't allow much sun in. The wallpaper looks as if it would have been a weighty struggle to hang, all texture and deep colours. The furniture could never be rearranged, even for a cozy card game, by the frail sitters who quietly occupy the room on these sleepy afternoons. Some have visitors, one woman always reads. The teacups click on the saucers.

When Mrs. Lefort first asked me to play the small pump organ that lives opposite the massive black fireplace, I felt intrusive, but I quickly lost myself in the music and the rhythmic motion of my feet. Now it has become a ritual part of my visits. Mrs. Lefort says the other ladies find the music very soothing, and I feel as if I'm reaching Mother in a way that no other interaction does. Maybe we are communicating in the only language we have left. I play a little Bach, maybe a few hymns, always Belmont, which used to make Dad cry. When I have run out of things to play we go back to her room together. She needs to rest.

Mother's changed behaviour puzzled me for a long time. Her doctor explained that some sufferers of senile dementia experience an altered perception of time and therefore an altered perception of their place in the continuum of their own life. Memory becomes present tense. But I wanted to know where she was, not why she had gone there. I intruded into one of her journeys when I arrived to visit on a particularly hot July afternoon. Mother was sitting in her rocking chair by the closed and curtained window. She was speaking to her mirror.

"Don't go in there, Barbie. You know what happens. You'll be sorry." Her voice was sing-songy but with an edge of anxiety. I assumed she was thinking of my sister. "Papa's coming and if he catches you up there you'll be in big trouble."

"Where is she going?" I couldn't help but ask, just to see what would happen. She turned her head sharply, surprised.

"Mabel? Is that you? I thought you'd never get here. I've been waiting and waiting."

"I'm not Mabel. I'm Ruth."

"Ruth?" She seemed genuinely puzzled. "Ruth." Her face was a complete blank, pale and smooth, free from worry lines, eyes wide and seeing some other world. But she couldn't see me. "Your daughter."

She laughed out loud then, as if I'd told her the silliest story, the most preposterous lie. Then she turned back to the mirror.

"Mabel's here now, Barbie. I don't care what you say anymore. Everything's all right now that Mabel's here." She closed her eyes and let her hands rest together in her lap.

She's sitting in that position now, having had her exercise, and her music, and her tea. I can't tell if she's sleeping or just pretending to. I have a book to read, but find myself drawn to the photographs on the wall. I brought them from the house when Mother first moved in to Mrs. Lefort's, and have tried to use them as some kind of atlas, a guide to how she orients herself. I notice one photograph of Dad and Uncle Harold, leaning against Dad's first car under the huge maple tree that shaded part of the barnyard. I remember a conversation I had with Harold that helped me start to see a little light in Mother's foggy world.

"Your mother's reminding me more and more of her mother, you know," Harold had said. He'd been in the middle of a repair job on one of the tractors and he wiped his hands methodically on a once-white rag. "She was real prim and proper. Not like the other women in her family."

Harold is the son who took over the family dairy farm. He and my father had agreed that since Dad had a family he would live in the big house, and Harold built a smaller house on the property, right at the corner where the lane turned to climb the grade to our yard. We lived on the farm, but didn't farm it. My father was a schoolteacher. "What'samatter, John, don'tcha like cows?" his neighbours teased him. "That's the problem," he would say, smiling, "I never met a cow I didn't like." And that was what it always came to.

"They were quite a crowd," Harold continued. I thought he

had left our conversation, but apparently he was only ruminating. "Your dad and me used to spend time over their place quite a bit, growing up. You see, your mother's aunt Sadie was married to our mother's cousin, so it was all kind of in the family."

I knew the story, having had the connections carefully explained to me by my father. He firmly believed that all personal troubles could be traced to family relationships. "It's all repeating patterns," he would say, and I would imagine his high school history students pencilling those words in the margins of their chapter on Napoleon or Hitler.

"'Our town cousins' we called them." Harold chewed again, the long, green stalk of timothy waving as he shifted sides. He seemed to be considering the cumulus clouds that had arisen over the barn roof during the afternoon. I wondered if he was remembering the lightning that had struck the original. "Your grandmother kept a tight tether on those girls, made them wear starched collars and kept them busy with the cleaning and so on, though they always had a hired girl. It was a sight to see them lined up on Sunday, trying so hard not to giggle, and she'd be there beside them, ready to smack the leg of the first one to snort when Reverend Henderson came up the aisle."

"Do you think I'll end up like Mother?" I asked Harold, interrupting his memory because I was suddenly gripped by a panic I wanted someone to ease. He and I had become allies in the years since Dad's death, the only two in the family without partners and children.

Harold put a heavy arm across my shoulders. "Maybe you will," he said. "Maybe you already have. But I sure wouldn't go thinkin' too hard on it, if I was you." He left my side and went off over the hill for the cows. He only needed to open the gate where they waited and they would plod, unguided, along the muddy path and back to their barn as they had done every afternoon of their lives. Harold had told me he would only do the chores for another year. He was planning his retirement.

"Who moved that photograph?" Mother's sharp voice breaks into my thoughts. She has finished resting. "I'm sure it was that cleaning girl. We just can't trust any of them." She touches the picture of herself and her five sisters. It was taken the day of Grandma Laurence's funeral. I was nine years old when she finally had the stroke that killed her. I remember her daughters, all but two of them dead now, gathered in our kitchen after the service. They laughed. I was so surprised, expecting sad faces and dark dresses like in my books. But here were these grown women laughing, as if they had shared a huge joke, a merry secret kept hidden from everyone else. Barbara stayed in the house that afternoon, but Dad and Uncle Harold took me out to the barn with them at milking time. I rode on Uncle Harold's shoulders. The cows were warm and there was a new litter of kittens in the hay mow, tucked safely into their nest. They were utterly lost when their mother stood up and moved away from them. They crawled blindly around in circles, bumping and mewing.

Mother seems to have forgotten her concern about the photograph's proper place and now she has begun to tidy, randomly moving the objects on her dresser and wiping away imaginary dust. I always consider this to be a sign that she is bored with my presence. Perhaps it's just my way of finding a reason other than my own anxiety for leaving.

"I think it's time I was heading home now, Mother," I tell her.

She turns her head quickly, as if surprised to find someone else in her room. "Leaving?" she looks puzzled. "Don't you live here too?"

"No, I have my own place. Just down the road. I'll be back again on Tuesday."

When I step out through the double front doors and hear them clunk firmly behind me I feel the wind from the marsh and breathe it in like tonic.

On the way home I pull the car onto the sandy shoulder and

walk along the cart track that leads to the marsh. Ahead of me I can see the place we always called The Island, though it has not been surrounded by water since the dykes were built, centuries ago. Still, the round hill covered in scrub pine remnant rises above the flat land, cut off from the bay, but close enough to have its farthest edge eroded by high spring tides. Now it seems to be encircled in a sea of sweet clover.

I climb over the last barbed-wire barrier and find myself among the herd of cows that is always grazing here, where the mud-red water is a stone's throw away. The slow clouds and the ripples sparkling in the slanting sunlight are the same as they always have been, the same as on the long afternoons when Barbara and I would come out to sketch cows and trees, the same as the day Mother and I came to scatter Dad's ashes in the tidal current. I take a few deep breaths and close my eyes, letting the ebb wash out the lost time, then I head back.

Fledglings

SHANNON KERNAGHAN

LAUREL HEARS a thud and turns from the stove knowing, without looking, that it's the dull clap of a bird hitting the window. The kitchen has the only window without dangling chimes or lengths of shiny ribbon, anything to deter their flight path.

She's surprised to see the flash of a hawk's wing against the glass, and watches it fly high into the branches of her maple tree. The hawk soars evenly, and based on the sound of the impact, Laurel figures it only glanced off the glass.

A feather, she thinks, *maybe it's dropped a feather for me.* She hurries outside and slides her bare feet through damp grass until she reaches the garbage cans.

Laurel discovers no hawk feather. Instead she finds a young sparrow below the window, feet up with tail feathers supported by her garden hose. Its tiny chest heaves, bouncing its claws in fast motion.

"Dirty hawk," she says in the tree's direction, realizing that while the hawk is unharmed, it's the fledgling that smeared fluff and a streak of beak wetness onto her window pane. Before inspecting the sparrow, she starts towards her maple, ready to shout and flail her arms to chase the hawk away. She stops. The hawk is simply doing what comes naturally. Nature's menu happens to include fledglings hatched in the birdhouse her ex-fiancé built. She eats every meal at the same chair, the one with the best vantage point. It delights her to watch the birds flit back and forth from a feeder to their roost atop a high pole outside her dining-room window. It makes her third of the rental house feel more like a home.

Her initial plan was for songbirds to fill the air with colour and melody, but raucous sparrows showed up first. Watching them squabble, mate, and survive is comforting to Laurel. With their distinctive personalities and hierarchies, they've stayed in control of their six-holed condo ever since.

Kneeling in the wet grass, she bends over the bird to assess the damage. It doesn't stir and still gasping, stares in her direction with eyes wide open.

"What should I do with you, baby? I can't watch you die like this," she whispers. Images of the rain barrel swirl through her mind, where she can hold it below the water's surface until air bubbles fail to rise. But the wing flapping, or any form of struggle, will be too upsetting.

Or she can find an old towel and a blunt hammer. One blow to its soft body, with green bones hardly formed, will be enough to release the bird from its suffering. Laurel has trouble with the subject of suffering. She stopped her newspaper subscription and cancelled her cable TV, anything to slow the steady diet of local, national, even international gloom and tragedy. At twenty-four, she knows it's denial, yet rationalizes that the extra time leaves her more chance to study.

"So I'm a little ignorant of world events," she tells friends in the Far Side Lounge at school. "Psych classes and English lit keep me plenty busy."

The flutter of wings causes her head to turn. It's the hawk, leaving her yard in search of other bird morsels and down-covered rabbits.

Each time her hand nears the sparrow, she stops and pulls back her arm. In shock from its flight of terror and then the collision with glass, its pinprick eyes blink but don't react to her presence. Laurel decides to do nothing, staying out of nature's way entirely, and goes inside to prepare for the visit.

The visit is a weekly excursion to see her grandfather who went into a nursing home last year. The family said "went into" although Gramps used words like "sabotaged" and "dumped." Outnumbered and overpowered, he refused to make any preparations besides packing his small travel bag with toiletries, one framed photo of his wife, and several copies of *Reader's Digest*.

"You sort out this junk if you're so damn anxious to get rid of me."

A widower for years, his family did their best to keep him in his own home for as long as possible. After too many falls from ladders and curbs, Gramps entered the Red Deer Nursing Home at eighty. He didn't want to go, and never missed the opportunity to complain. "I'll strike you ungrateful upstarts from my will," and "Who are you to lock me in and throw away the key? I changed all your goddamned diapers!"

It wasn't true, he'd never touched a diaper in his life, clean or dirty. But it always upset Laurel to think he'd felt abandoned.

It wasn't easy for Laurel's parents either. They had little time to spare within their real estate careers, and no extra room in their condominium. Overnight, Gramps had become high-maintenance.

Laurel considered moving in with him, but it didn't materialize. It all happened in the middle of breaking up with her fiancé. By the time she made the decision, Gramps had already been panelled by the care home and placed on the waiting list. Thanks to a high rate of pneumonia over the winter, he moved quickly to the head of the line.

"Only damn line I've been in that moved too fast," he muttered, loud enough for all to hear when they walked him down the steps of his family home for the final time.

"Hi, Gramps, how's it going?" Laurel calls softly into his ear. His vitriol has lessened over the past year, along with his vigour. Opening his eyes, he smiles when he sees Laurel. She reaches under the mohair blanket and finds his hand, thin fingers of chalk. The old man's grip is strong and he holds her hand tightly. "How they treating you?"

"Same old," and he struggles into a sitting position. She assists by pulling his wrist. "Hey, not so hard, you trying to break my arm?"

"Sorry, just helping." He grins and she mock-slaps his shoulder. "Aren't *you* the comedian today," and she kisses his forehead. "Where's your comb?" At some point during his adaptation to nursing-home living, a tradition had begun. When Laurel arrives for her afternoon visit, the first thing she does is comb his remaining hair, silky white wisps matted in an upward swoop resulting from his frequent naps.

"I saw it by the sink," he says, staring out the low window across from his bed. "Or maybe that was yesterday." She positions his walker next to the bed, within reach. "Whatya bring me?"

"What am I? A walking vending machine?" she calls out. In the bathroom she smiles at her reflection while running warm water through his comb. It's the same every Friday — she rolls out of bed dreading the visit but when there, she can't imagine not being with him. "Reach into my bag next to you. I brought you some Wagon Wheels and oranges and chips —"

"Old Dutch Rip-L? You know I only like Old Dutch —"

"Yes, Gramps, Old Dutch Rip-L, I know." When she returns, she finds the snacks as well as her school books and contents of her makeup bag scattered across his bed. "You haven't asked how my courses are going."

"You still in school? Aren't you ever gonna get a job?" He's already opened the chips and half-peeled an orange. "How old are you now, forty?"

"Very funny. Hey, spread it out, Gramps, you'll get sick if you eat everything now." He nods but struggles with the hard white plastic on a cookie. Before he can eat more, she gathers the remains and stows it inside his bedside drawer. "Save some for tonight or you'll spoil your supper." He doesn't argue and Laurel takes her spot next to him on the edge of the bed.

She starts at his temple, gently pulling the comb past his ear. She moves slowly since his hair is fine, like combing a child's head. It doesn't need much, merely shaping, and he enjoys it, closing his eyes and tilting his head downwards.

Laurel has to initiate conversation. He answers but if she doesn't speak, he does nothing more than gaze towards his window or root through his drawers for something to eat. His internal mealtime clock is non-existent.

"Did I tell you that a hawk chased a sparrow into my kitchen window today? It was still alive when I left but it didn't look too good."

"The hawk?"

"No, the fledgling. It'll probably be dead when I get home."

"You never know. Hardy creatures, all of us. I'll come by later and hang something in your window, I've got the tools."

"Thanks, Gramps," she says, humouring him. "That's a good idea." She makes a part down the middle. "After all the rain, everything is so green outside your window. And smell that air, isn't it fresh? It almost has a taste to it."

He's silent, already tiring, and gives one nod in agreement. After setting down the comb, she begins to rub his shoulders with light strokes.

"You're falling asleep, how about taking a nap?" He opens his eyes for a moment.

"Might as well, I can't dance." Laurel has no idea what he means even though she's heard that declaration since her earliest memory of him, memories that include aqua-coloured Easter eggs, nickel- and dime-filled birthday cakes, and lazy days floating on inner tubes at the family lakeside cabin. It always makes her smile. He should have that motto etched onto his headstone. But it's not something you say to a man over eighty.

"After age seventy," he told Laurel on his sixty-ninth birthday, "you're livin' on borrowed time. Never forget that." At twelve, Laurel's options seemed limitless. At twenty-four, her crystal ball has grown hazy.

She eases his head onto the pillow and shifts his legs into a comfortable position.

"Have a nice snooze, Gramps, I'll be here when you wake up." He nods, his eyes already closed. "Gramps?" His eyes open again. "I love you."

"I love you too, dear."

Laurel senses her finite opportunity to tell him how she feels. Usually "I love you" is her parting line when she says goodbye for the week.

Without making a sound, Laurel lifts a chair and places it next to his bed before opening a book. She doesn't read more than a page when another resident begins to shout from the hallway. Laurel recognizes the voice, that of a feisty woman from the next room. With all of four teeth in her head, Oxana is notorious for her guttural outbursts emphasized by a strong European accent. Gramps doesn't stir but when the shouting increases in volume, Laurel tiptoes to shut his door. As she swings around to return, the woman roars out a high-pitched shriek.

Laurel then watches her grandfather catapult off his bed from a sleeping position. In his T-shirt and pyjama bottom, he topples over his walker. The speed of his movement propels his body along in these sickening split seconds. He only stops when his head rams against the concrete wall.

By the time Laurel reacts, Gramps is already on the ground with his hand reaching for the side of his head. Face up, his brown eyes stare towards the ceiling. He doesn't try to move, lucky since his sock-covered feet are tangled in the walker.

"Gramps!" Laurel yells, and then speaks quietly. "Gramps, stay there, let me get someone to ... to make sure you're all right." Since his neck is slumped in an awkward position against the wall, she slips a pillow carefully between his head and the floor. "I'm going to get Jake, to make sure you haven't broken anything. *Promise* you'll stay put, okay Gramps?" He says nothing and continues to stare, now with a grimace of pain pulling up the corners of his mouth. Thick spittle drools down his chin, but she can't wait, she has to find the nurse.

She flies down the hall, calling out, "Jake! Jake, where are you?" Minutes before the accident she heard his voice giving instructions outside the door, something about "doing Elsie's fleet."

She finds only residents scattered along the walls of the hall-way, watching Laurel with dull eyes and stooped shoulders from their wheelchairs and walkers as she darts into several rooms along her path. The only sound is from the slapping of her sandals.

"What am I thinking?" she says to no one, and races back to the room. Relieved, yet equally worried to see that Gramps hasn't tried to pull himself up, she yanks the call cord and hurries to his side. Blood has oozed onto the pillow like a red nimbus. More blood is smeared across his fingers from where he's touched his wound. "How are you doing? Are you in much pain?"

"That's hard concrete," he says, still looking at a spot in the distance and then at his fingers.

"Leave it alone, wait 'til a nurse looks at it. Oh, Gramps, this is all my fault, how did I let you fall?"

"Don't worry," he says and reaches for her hand. "By tomor-row I'll forget this ever happened."

Laurel wants to throw the folded walker at the toothless hag who continues to screech from her room; she wants to ask why he flew out of bed like a crazy man, and how he ejected himself with such speed; and she wants to scream at herself for leaving the walker in his path. If she hadn't fussed about shutting the door, she could have reached out and easily caught his shoulders when he began his launch. It would have been a non-incident and she'd still be reading about the deformities of Alexander Pope instead of kneeling by Gramps's bloody pillow and wanting to cry, or vomit, or both. From ground level she notices yellow streaks across the floor and hopes it's nothing more than dried orange juice. She then looks at the shape of his fingers and narrow nails, surprised she never realized how much they resemble hers. Using the pulse banging at her temples to count the seconds, Laurel hears footsteps approaching.

Jake, the LPN, enters quickly, followed by two women.

"What's the problem here, Tony? Hi, Laurel, looks like he's had a spill. Don't move, Tony," he says loudly, forgetting that Gramps's hearing is one of the few things that still work. Jake manipulates legs and arms, searching for pain. "Looks like your grandpa got a good bonkus of the conkus. Dumb place for a concrete wall, hey Tony?"

"You can say that again," Gramps whispers, a small broken doll when they raise him onto the bed.

Laurel sits on one side, gripping his hand, and Jake on the other, pushing the hair away to inspect his injury. "It won't need stitches, just a bandage. You might have a little headache, Tony. Flo, go and get me an ice pack, please. I'll finish his vitals." His hands move swiftly, calmly. "It's time for you to check on Elsie's fleet," he says to the other aide who flashes an expression like she'd prefer to be anywhere else at that moment.

Laurel explains what happened while Jake observes her grandfather's blood pressure and listens to his heart rate.

"Look over here, Tony ... no, this way, that's good. I think he'll be okay, it doesn't look too bad."

"I bet you're glad I came to visit. I leave him for two seconds and he gets hurt. Great help I am."

"Yeah, what are you, a jinx or something?" Jake smiles at her. "You've had lots of falls, haven't you, Tony. You're a tough guy."

"I feel no pain. What are we having for supper?" Gramps says and begins to reach for his bowl of peanuts on the side table.

"I didn't read the board but something smells good out there. Laurel, would you like to hold this against his head for fifteen minutes, to keep down the swelling? And how do you spell your last name? It's for my report."

"Morris, same as Tony."

"Right. I'll be back to check on him. By the way, I like your new hair style. See ya later, jinx. And you take it easy, Tony."

She helps Gramps onto his side and positions the ice pack gently on his wound. Her lower lip begins to quiver and she bites it, refusing to break down. She promises to let herself fall apart later.

"I think he likes you," Gramps says.

"Who, Jake? Nah, he's just being friendly. He is kinda cute ... hey, stop worrying about me and tell me why you flew out of bed like a crazy man?"

"I heard a scream, I thought it was your grandma. When you marry Jake, tell him my hearing's fine, it's my head that hurts."

Laurel lets out a choked burst of laughter and smoothes his ruffled hair. With a wet cloth, she wipes lightly at the streak of blood on his neck. She kisses his forehead and stays near his side.

When she returns home, Laurel heads for her chair in the dining room, but changes her mind after noticing that the bird feeder is empty. It's then that she remembers the fledgling.

The bird is gone without a trace, not even a soft feather to mark where it landed. "I hope this means the hawk didn't come back for your baby, at least not today," she says to the sparrows that hover within range when she pours seed into the top of the feeder. She hardly sets the lid back in place when several dive from the air, competing for the two feeding perches.

Laurel stays in the yard to watch them eat. She drops into the cool grass after kicking off her sandals, and gazes up at the pale evening sky. The need to cry has passed; she thinks of her grandfather's nails and stares at her own outstretched fingers. *Hardy creatures, all of us.*

She decides to watch some TV, even though she's down to three channels. Tonight she can handle a little world news.

Acknowledgements

Emily Schultz would like to thank Sumach Press (all of you!) for the expertise, time, and patience put into this project. Thanks also to the contributors, who lent me their stories to play with; I hope I'm returning them still in one piece. Thanks also to Brian Joseph Davis for the stunning cover photographs and for making me pull off the 401 for ten o'clock bingo; Mary Newberry for advice and last-minute favours; Kitty Lewis at Brick Books; and, lastly, Viviane Kertesz for listening to me complain about everything-that-could-have-gone-wrong. Thank you.

N

Kelly Cooper's story "N. Loves Peggy" was first published in *Windsor ReView* (Spring 1999). Reprinted by permission of the author.

Melanie Little's story "Carmen: The Idea of Red" was first published in *Event* (Summer 2001). Reprinted by permission of the author.

Liza Potvin's story "Assumptions" was first published in *Zygote* (Winter 2000). Reprinted by permission of the author.

Emily Schultz's story "The Years of the Strawberry Circus" was first published in *Blood & Aphorisms* (Summer 1999). Reprinted by permission of the author.

Sybil Shaw-Hamm's story "To Dance in a Measured Space" was first published in *NeWest Review* (Summer 1997). Reprinted by permission of the author.

Contributors

TAMMY ARMSTRONG'S writing has appeared in numerous literary magazines and anthologies in Canada, the US, and the UK. She is the recipient of the New Brunswick Writers Federation Alfred G. Bailey Prize, the David Adams Richards Prize, and placed third in the League of Canadian Poets National Poetry Award 2001. Her first collection of poetry is *Bogman's Music* (Anvil Press, 2001). Her first novel, *Translations: Aistreann*, will be published spring 2002 (Coteau Books). She grew up in St. Stephen, New Brunswick (population 5,000), where she dreamt of bookstores and movie theatres. Now in Vancouver, she is currently writing a new novel and going to the movies too often.

KELLY COOPER works as an art teacher and makes her home on a dairy farm in Belleisle Creek, New Brunswick. She has been published in literary journals across Canada and was the winner of The Fiddlehead's Fiction Prize and the Short Grain Contest in the spring of 2001. Her work has been included in a number of anthologies, the most recent of which are *Entering the Landscape: Revisioning Nature in Canadian Fiction* (Oberon, 2001) and *The Mentor's Canon* (Broken Jaw Press, 2001).

KAREN HANLON lives in Quispamsis, New Brunswick, near the Kennebecasis River, with her husband and two teenage daughters. She was brought up in southern Ontario, outside of Guelph, but has lived in the Maritimes for the past twenty-five years. She is a former nurse. Karen writes short fiction and is currenly working on a historical novel that is set in New Brunswick. Her work has won several prizes in the Writer's Federation of New Brunswick's annual writing competition. Lately she has been finding great pleasure in "ghost-writing" autobiographies.

ANGELA HRABOWIAK forgets to be good. She is irreverent and orange — tangy, round and juicy. She explores her Ukrainian cultural past and Canadian rural roots through her writing and painting. She lives in Hamilton, Ontario — a wonderful city, combining accessible rural pleasures with modern big city "cultural events" — about twenty miles from where she grew up. Part of a women's writing group, she has published locally. The small space she writes from is her memory or perception of reality, which she explores more as she becomes braver in her writing.

JOANNE K. JEFFERSON grew up in Halifax and now lives with her partner, two young sons, three cats, and a dog on the shore of the LaHave River in southwestern Nova Scotia. She has been writing poetry, fiction, and drama since she was in grade school, and is trying to make a living as a freelance magazine writer and editor. Joanne's poems have been published in *Gaspereau Review, Undertow,* and *Critical Mass* (now *Henry Street*). Her interview with Governor General's Award winner George Elliott Clarke appeared in a recent issue of *Atlantic Books Today.*

SHANNON KERNAGHAN is the author of *Like Minds* (New Muse Award for Short Fiction, 1998) and *How to Sell Your Home Privately* (self-help). She rants and reflects in a weekly column for the *Red Deer Advocate.* Shannon has called four provinces home and currently lives in Alberta. Central Alberta's dominating influence is its strong sense of community. Each varying landscape — from coastal to prairie, from large to small — has added fresh dimensions to her writing.

K. LINDA KIVI is a rural British Columbia writer, naturalist and jill-of-all-trades. Her books include the novel *If Home is a Place* (Polestar Press, 1995) and the creative documentaries *Canadian Women Making Music* (Green Dragon Press, 1992), and *Fidelity* (Maa Press, 1999). The story "Mermaids" is contrived from a biographical snippet about the nineteenth-century Newfoundland opera diva whose stage name was Marie Toulingette.

MELANIE LITTLE's fiction and essays have appeared in *The Malahat Review, subTerrain, Event, Books in Canada,* and *The Vancouver Sun,* as well as in the anthologies *Scribner's Best of the Fiction Workshops* and *Nerves Out Loud* (Annick Press). She won the Writers Union of Short Prose Competition in 1997 and was runner-up for the 2001 Bronwen Wallace Award. Her first book, a collection of stories, will be published by Thomas Allen Publishers in 2003. She grew up in Timmins, Ontario, and did not know Shania Twain. Currently, she lives in Ottawa.

KATHY MAGHER writes from Toronto, where she's been published in *The Writing Space Journal* and *ink magazine.* "The Medicine Cabinet" is part of a collection of short stories she's working on. Kathy grew up in Frampton, in the beautiful Beauce region of Quebec.

LIZA POTVIN is the author of *White Lies (for my mother),* published by NeWest Press in 1992. It won the Edna Staebler Award for Creative

Nonfiction. She has a book of short fiction *Flights of Gravity* forthcoming with Raincoast Books. She teaches at Malaspina University-College in Nanaimo, British Columbia.

KIM SCARAVELLI's first stories were crayon loop-the-loops on construction paper pages. In college, she conformed to black on white, writing a humour column for *The Dalhousie Gazette* before the need to earn a living tossed her in a different direction. Several careers later, she is at home with two young children and lots of crayons. She gets up at an hour when only the crows and she have the gall to flap about, and writes with pure joy. Her sarcastic musings were recently heard on CBC Radio. She is now working on the rewrites of her first novel.

SYBIL SHAW-HAMM was born and raised in Saskatchewan. Her adult life has been spent in Manitoba, raising three children, working as a nurse, and as a social and peace activist. She is privileged to have retired to the bush in southern Manitoba to learn to write. Her short stories have been published in *Prairie Fire, NeWest Review, Other Voices, Zygote, Free Fall, Room of One's Own,* and anthologies by McMaster University, Canadian Summer Games, Rowan Books, and Woodlake Books. Her collection of short stories is looking for a home. Her novel is a work in progress.

BETSY TRUMPENER lives below Tabor Mountain, east of Prince George, British Columbia. Her life on the outskirts has included time in Iowa City, U.S.A.; Quesnel, British Columbia; Peterborough, Ontario; and St. Peter, Germany. Betsy's fiction and nonfiction have been published in *The Malahat Review, Event, THIS Magazine,* and *NOW* Magazine, broadcast on CBC Radio, and anthologized in *Exact Fare Only* (Anvil Press). Betsy is CBC Radio's news reporter for northern British Columbia.

GAÏTANE VILLENEUVE grew up in Glovertown, Newfoundland, and is a graduate of St. Thomas University. She is currently working on a collection of short stories that span fifty years, focusing on the lives of a connected group of people in a small Newfoundland outport. "Wire Basket" is the first story in that collection. She now lives in Canada's Arctic with her husband, Patrick Feltham, and their dog, Larkin.

REBECCA McCLELLAN

EMILY SCHULTZ grew up in Wallaceburg, Ontario (population 11,500), and now has a love-hate relationship with Toronto. Her own short story collection *Black Coffee Night* is forthcoming (Insomniac Press). She is currently writing a novel set in a fictional small town at the onset of the video-game era. She wrote "The Years of the Strawberry Circus" while in Windsor, Ontario, attaining her BA. It was first published in *Blood & Aphorisms,* and was selected for this collection by the publisher.